G. W. Dasent

The Vikings of the Baltic

Vol. 1

Anatiposi

G. W. Dasent

The Vikings of the Baltic

Vol. 1

Reprint of the original, first published in 1875.

1st Edition 2024 | ISBN: 978-3-38282-889-9

Anatiposi Verlag is an imprint of Outlook Verlagsgesellschaft mbH.

Verlag (Publisher): Outlook Verlag GmbH, Zeilweg 44, 60439 Frankfurt, Deutschland
Vertretungsberechtigt (Authorized to represent): E. Roepke, Zeilweg 44, 60439 Frankfurt, Deutschland
Druck (Print): Books on Demand GmbH, In de Tarpen 42, 22848 Norderstedt, Deutschland

THE

VIKINGS OF THE BALTIC

A Tale of the North in the Tenth Century.

BY

G. W. DASENT, D.C.L.,

AUTHOR OF "ANNALS OF AN EVENTFUL LIFE," ETC.

IN THREE VOLUMES.

VOL. I.

LONDON:
CHAPMAN AND HALL, 193, PICCADILLY.
1875.

NOTICE.

THE events related in the following story are in the main historical. It cannot be gainsaid that towards the close of the tenth century a formidable free company of Vikings, or sea-rovers, had established themselves, under laws of their own, in an impregnable fortress on the shore of the Baltic, at the mouth of the Oder. No less certain is it that, first under the captainship of their founder, Palnatoki, and after his death under that of Sigvald, the son of Strut-Harold, those free-booters were a thorn in the side of the Wendish kings on whose soil their stronghold lay, and still more in that of the kings of Denmark, from whose subjects that famous company was for the most part recruited. Jomsburg was an asylum for all the bold spirits and dashing blades of the time, and every man who joined the band was so much strength taken from the vigour of the land to which he by birth belonged. Besides, in the case of Denmark there were added wrongs received and grudges harboured, not so much by the people as by the royal house. In the days of Harold Bluetooth, not only had Palnatoki fostered and backed Sweyn, his outlaw son, but his unerring arrow had slain King Harold himself, and thus thrown on Sweyn the sacred duty of revenge. More than this, Sweyn was hardly seated on his father's throne than he was seized by Sigvald, who in the meantime had succeeded Palnatoki as captain of the company, and carried off to Jomsburg, where he was forced against his will to marry a Wendish princess.

Equally certain it is, that at the solemn funeral ale, or feast of heirship, which Sigvald, by the customs of his race and age, was bound to hold on the occasion of his father's death, King Sweyn, finding himself too weak to cope openly with the Vikings, led them on, when they were wild with drink, to make rash vows, which bound them to attack Hacon, the mighty Earl of Norway; and thus to embark on an expedition which cut off the flower of their company, and so brought about the ruin of Jomsburg.

It must be observed, however, that modern criticism, while allowing the truth of each of the events narrated in the story, has, for good reasons of its own, thought it right to arrange them in a somewhat different order, and thus to disturb that natural sequence according to which we find them described in the Saga of the Vikings of Jomsburg, which may be read in the original in the eleventh volume of the "Fornmanna Sögur." But while we bow in matters of critical history to such authorities as Munch and Dahlmann, it is enough for our present purpose to point out the fact that the poetic treatment of the story of these Vikings, as it was rounded into shape in the Icelandic of the fourteenth century, has a truth and warmth and beauty of its own which far outweigh the worth of any historical skeleton, however carefully its dry bones may have been collected and strung together.

For this reason the Saga of the Vikings of Jomsburg has been followed as a guide in this story, in which it is hoped that something may be found of the strength and spirit with which the wonderful adventures of that famous company are narrated in the original. Having said so much, the work must speak for itself. If it should persuade any reader to turn to that great storehouse of literature of which the Icelandic language holds the key, and to prove for himself what is historical and what fiction in these volumes, the writer will be well repaid. He has taken the liberty to put a free translation of the famous Dirge on King Eric Bloody-axe into the mouth of the Skald Einar Scaleclang, and to apply it to the death of Erlend, Hacon's son. A few lines quoted from memory out of the poems of his dear friend John Sterling, have also been given to the same Icelandic Skald.

CONTENTS.

THE

VIKINGS OF THE BALTIC.

CHAPTER I.

HOW JOMSBURG AROSE.

Now we must go away from this nineteenth century, with its manners and customs, its Devastations and Ruperts, and Armstrong and Palliser guns, far, far away into the North, in the tenth century, with its bows and arrows and broad axes and spears. You do not care to follow me ? Oh yes, you will ; for this will be a very amusing story, full of perilous ventures and hairbreadth escapes, and so utterly different from your humdrum and everyday existence—for I will not call it life—that the mere contrast must be as refreshing to you as a dose of quinine to a fever-stricken man on the Gold Coast.

There is no question, therefore, of going or

not going. You are to follow whither I lead you, and in an instant, quicker even than the flash of the electric spark, time and space are suspended, and you are standing with me within the walls of Jomsburg, on the east shore of the Baltic, in the last quarter of the tenth century of the Christian æra. And now, before the story begins, do let me beg you to shake off all that cant of conventionalities called civilization, and forgetting all the prejudices which have been engendered in your nature in all the ages between this and the tenth century, enter fully and freely into the life and being of the men and women whom you are about to meet.

Jomsburg was a castle, that the ending -borg or -burg implies; but what was Jom? I am afraid the answer must be left in doubt. Whether it were the name of a man or of a place, there in the tenth century stood the castle, not far from the modern Wollin in Pomerania. That part of Germany, as we should now call it, was then held by the Wends, for the most part a heathen Sclavonic race, whose name still lingers in the Wends in Lusatia, as well as in the title which the King of Sweden takes as Lord of "the Goths and Vandals." The names of the Wendish kings in those days were very Sclavonic, and very jaw-breaking. Burislaf is the easiest of them, and Mieczyslaf not nearly the hardest. In this story they will trouble us little; a fact which I announce with great satisfaction both to my readers and myself. Who can read a tale of fiction with any comfort out loud when utterance is attended with the probable loss of one's front teeth? A very short course of these Wendish names would turn a man into a confirmed stutterer for life. But if we are not to use Wendish names, how can we write of a Wendish castle? Did not Burislaf own it? No, he did not. He was Lord paramount of Jomsburg indeed, but quite another race held it, and that was why the name sounds so easy. Jomsburg was a castle held by a band of Scandinavian sea-rovers, who used it as an asylum for themselves and their ill-gotten or well-gotten goods. They had seized it and fortified it without the leave of the Lord paramount, who, not being strong enough to turn the intruders out, did the next best thing, made friends with them, accepted the situation, and looked at last on the Jomsburgers in the light rather of friends than enemies, and as the garrison of a stronghold which kept off worse enemies. On their part, the sea-rovers or Vikings forebore to waste or harry the Wendish lands; their hands were against every man but the subjects of the Wendish King, and so at last they were regarded as friends rather than foes, and as a source of strength instead of weakness to the Wendish King.

When we talk of a castle, we are not to rush off with our fourteenth century notions of a graceful structure like Carnarvon or Conway. It was no Edwardian pile that Palnatoki, for that was the name of their first captain, built for his Vikings on the Baltic coast. They were sea-rovers, and as he pushed along the low sandy Wendish shore, he spied out an inlet in that tideless sea into which he could always run his galleys, and which would hold 300 ships. His first need was a constant depth of water and a land-locked harbour, and this he found at Jom or Jomi. All round the inlet he threw a wall or curtain of cyclopean architecture; huge ramparts more than thirty feet high, and of immense thickness. Here and there on the wall were low towers, out of which the garrison could look landward, though, as we have seen, as time went on, there was little need to look for an inland attack. It was from the sea that the Vikings expected enemies, and the defences at the mouth of the harbour were very strong. It was there that the Vaubans of Jomsburg exhausted all their devices. Across the narrow entrance, which would only admit one ship at a time, a rude arch was turned, and under it, as ship followed ship lowering her single mast, they shot into the smooth water of the haven. Over this portal was raised the only approach to a castle which Jomsburg possessed. It was tall and massive, and shapeless, built out into the sea on either side of the arch and towering above it in two stories. Woe betide the war galley that tried to force a way into that harbour, the entrance to which was further barred by booms and chains. In that tower were piled up huge stones, which might be suddenly dropped through slits in the masonry on the devoted vessel, as soon as she had reached the arch. Within these cyclopean walls the rovers or Vikings of that famous free company, the *condottieri* of the sea, lived in the wooden houses of the time, when they were not skimming the western waters in quest of booty and renown. They had arisen out of the turbulence of the time. Old things were passing away in the North, and the new were not yet established ; the ancient respect for the royal families and petty princes of the Scandinavian kingdoms was waning, and in the attempt to establish dynasties the Kings of Denmark, Sweden, and Norway had abandoned for the most part the duty of leading their adventurous youth to expeditions by sea. They were too busy at home to care any longer for the harvest of the waves. The age of Ragnar Lodbrog was over, and the system of Harold Fairhair was yet in its infancy. The northern kingdoms were slowly taking constitutional shape and settling down into a new form ; but all over the north the old sea-roving spirit still burned in many bosoms with a fierce flame, and when their natural leaders failed them, free bands of Vikings arose, of which this famous company at Jomsburg was at once the foremost and most famous. These political causes were disturbing enough to throw the time out of gear and joint, but at the end of the tenth century a new root of discord was added, in those germs of the Christian belief, which, first sown by the Emperor Otho in Denmark, gradually spread over the whole North, but not without years of obstinate struggles and frequent apostacies.

So now we have arrived at some notion of Jomsburg and the Jomsburgers. It was a stronghold held with the tacit leave of the Wendish King, by a mighty band of free-booters, or Vikings, as they were then called. But we should much mistake the feelings which filled their breasts, and the ties which bound them together, if we imagined them to be a mere mass of vulgar pirates, only fit to be executed at the yard-arm. They were sea-rovers, because sea-roving was an honourable profession; just as much so as war in modern times, and this story will at least show that the Viking of the tenth century not only swept the seas and carried all before him, but that his career was full of ambition and of high enterprise.

Nor was it a band into which any warrior or

sea-rover might be enrolled for the asking. Very strict and searching were the enquiries in each case before admission to the band was allowed, and very stern were the conditions of remaining in it. In these respects it might be called a competitive examination, by which the way was opened to Jomsburg and the ranks of the sea-rovers recruited. No man might be older than thirty or younger than eighteen on admission. No one might stay in the company who yielded to a warrior equipped with the same arms as himself. Every man who entered was bound to make a solemn vow to avenge each of the others as he would his messmate or his own brother. No man was to slander one of the band, or to spread any news till its publication was sanctioned by the captain of the band. If he did so he was at once expelled. Even in the case of the paramount duty of that age, the sacred obligation to avenge a blood relation, if two such natural enemies met in the company, the captain was to settle what atonement should be made in money, and then the blood feud was to abate. All the spoil which the band took was to be shared in common, and if sold, sold for the good of all. If anyone was convicted of holding anything back he was to be at once expelled ; and if in any trouble or contest anyone so far forgot himself as to utter a word of complaint or fear, he was regarded as a coward and forced to leave the company. All admissions were to be decided by the valour and prowess of the applicant, and no considerations of kinship or favour were to be listened to. Last and not least, no one was to be absent from the castle longer than three nights without the captain's leave, and no woman was ever to be admitted into it.

Such were the articles of agreement under which the Vikings of Jomsburg, at once the terror and glory of the North, had been founded; and under these the band, which went out every summer to harry, returning in the winter to divide and enjoy their spoil, had won itself a name for prowess and hardihood, until it numbered amongst the brotherhood the boldest warriors of the North and West, and its name was synonymous with all that the Scandinavian race had to boast of in daring and renown.

CHAPTER II.

INSIDE THE BURG.

Now we are inside the burg. Below us is the land-locked harbour filled with the long-ships of the band. Behind us are the huge rough walls, and before us the loghouses built of timber of roughly squared fir-trees, in which the rank and file of the Vikings dwelt. Out of one of them appear close to us two of the band, one a man long passed fifty, and the other a lad, tall and strong, indeed, but whose youthful face hardly shows the eighteen summers which were needed for his election to the band. On all sides are groups of stalwart warriors, some tarring or painting their ships, some cleaning or polishing their arms. These are the axe, the bow, the sword, and the spear; except a steel hat or two, and very rarely a "byrnie" or shirt of linked mail, we see no defensive armour but the shield of oblong shape running down into a point. Making allowance for the change of times, the scene is not unlike the noise and hum of a modern dockyard.

We forgot to say that all round the wall, though at long intervals, stood sentinels, who, like those of our own time, spent their time idly for years, that they might be ready to give the alarm when some danger arose, and which in all probability would never come. Over the arch at the mouth of the haven stood a warder, with his horn ready to sound a blast of warning should any stranger approach the castle from the sea. But let us listen to what the two warriors nearest to us say.

"I tell you, foster-child," said the older man, "that this will never be for the good of the band. What would your grandfather, our founder, have said of such things? I say it again, the company is on the way to ruin. The laws should not be broken."

"They were broken when I came among you," said the younger, "and you break them now, Beorn, when you speak against the captain."

"Broken, indeed," said Beorn, looking at the lad with pride. "Broken, indeed, when you came among us. Did you not come here in your grandsire's time, just before he died, and did he not refuse to let you enter the band because you were too young? and did you not challenge our new captain Sigvald, him whom we now have, to single combat, outside the harbour, with two ships and one hundred picked men on each side? and did not Sigvald at last turn on his heel and fly before you? and then, did not all the band who, with your grandsire, looked on from the walls, declare that, though only sixteen, you were man enough for us when you could make one of our bravest warriors turn and fly? and so you were chosen to be one of us. That was breaking the law, it is true, and it is always bad to break the law; but this which our new captain Sigvald is going to do is breaking it in a worse way. If women once come within the castle, there is an end of Jomsburg and the Vikings.

"How do you know, foster-father, that the Captain has such things in his heart? One may know that a girl is lovely, and feel it, without bringing her into the Castle."

"Now, Vagn, my foster-child," said the old man with a chuckle, "you are thinking of that cruise of ours last summer to "the Bay" in Norway, when we harried Thorkell of Leira's land, and carried off his cattle and goods. You are thinking of Ingibeorg, that lovely lass whom we met in the wood the day we landed, and whom you would have carried off, only the law is, as the law ought to be, that no woman shall set her foot in Jomsburg, and so it ought to be. Vikings should have naught to do with women."

While Beorn was growling out these disrespectful things against the fair sex, a blush spread over the fair face of the young warrior, and it was easy to see from the mantling hue that he had not forgotten that fair Norwegian maiden. All he said was:

"We could not carry her off except to sell her as a slave, and that would have been too great an indignity even for the proud Thorkell; but enough of that. I say again, foster-father, what makes you say that the Captain is going to break the law?"

"One of these Wendish fellows told me," said the old man; "whether he were heathen or Christian I know not, but he said that the

Captain had sent word to King Burislaf that he wished to marry his daughter."

"Marry his daughter," burst out Vagn. "Then, if the Captain marries his daughter, the rest of the band might marry."

"And if they did, what would happen?" said the old Viking violently. "The castle would be filled with screaming women and squalling children. The good old Viking times are over, you know; you can't spit a baby now on a spear, or get rid of it in that way. We should all quarrel. The castle would be filled with gossip and slander. Tale-bearing would follow child-bearing. There will be no comfort, no peace; we shan't even be able to get our meals in peace."

"They would save us trouble in cooking," said Vagn.

"Cooking!" retorted Beorn. "My Welsh thrall Griffin will cook against all the women in the world, as you know well. But there's no use talking of it, foster-child; if the Captain breaks the law, there's an end to the glory of Jomsburg."

As he said this, two men came up to them;

both of commanding presence, and one tall beyond the stature of men.

"The glory of Jomsburg, Beorn," said the shorter of the two. "I hope the glory of Jomsburg will always be as great under my rule as under that of our founder Palnatoki. Nay! that it will be greater."

"Never praise the day, Sigvald, till it is over," said Beorn. "You are our Captain, and a brave one, but your rule is not over like that of Palnatoki. He is dead and gone, and he ever led us to victory and kept the law."

"Except when he broke it, Beorn," said the Captain, for it was he, as he pointed to Vagn with his axe.

"I wish," said Beorn, "that no one may ever break it for a worse cause. Sometimes, as the saw says, laws are made to be broken."

"So they are, Beorn," said the taller of the two, and I am sure my brother will never break them except for the common good."

"Tall as Yggdrasil's Ash, fair of face, glib of tongue, and strong as a bear," said Beorn. "So you are, and so you will ever be Thorkell the Tall; but for all that, you never will lay your bones in Jomsburg. That I can spae, without asking either the Christian God or Thorgerda Shrinebride, Earl Hacon's idol."

"Why so, Beorn?"

"Because you are too easy and yielding," said the veteran. "There is not a man among us who can reach farther with his axe; at one sweep of your sword men fly asunder, shorn through the middle, their head one way and their heels the other; with your bow, so long as your arrows last, you could keep off a host. The only man we have seen like you in these waters is the Icelander Gunnar of Lithend; but for all that you are too easily led astray. The Captain's brother, you ought to see that the laws of the company are kept."

"Come, Beorn," said Sigvald, "can you say that the company was ever so strong? last summer our war-snakes swarmed on the waters of the West. Thralls from Ireland, maids from Scotland, mead and cloth and honey from England, wine from France and Spain—have we not all these in Jomsburg? Had we ever more gallant men or braver ships? Is not Burislaf both afraid of us and proud of us. Afraid, lest we should become his foes, and proud of us as his friends?"

"Burislaf," growled out Beorn in disgust, more like the bear after which he was called than a human being.

"Why Burislaf?" asked Thorkell, imitating the growl in a way which made all the rest but Beorn laugh.

"Because I hate Burislaf and all his kin and race," said the old Viking. "First of all I hate to be at peace with any man or any thing, and we are always at peace with Burislaf. Our hands ought to be against every man, and ours are never against him. He lets us bide here in this asylum, and his bards call us his vassals."

"Vassals!" exclaimed the Captain. "Vassals! Pretty vassals who seized a town and held it against all comers, and a pretty liege lord who never dare come into his own town. We Vikings are King Burislaf's friends, and he is our friend. He loves us because no foes ever dare invade his coast so long as we hold Jomsburg, but we do not hold it of King Burislaf. It is our good swords that are our liege lords."

"Bravely spoken, and well spoken," said

Beorn; "but what I said to my foster-child Vagn here, I will say out boldly to you Captain. It is true that we were never stronger. Never, ever in the days of Palnatoki my foster-brother, was Jomsburg so full of spoil. It is not that. We are too prosperous perhaps; but it is the law that gets weaker among us, and by law, that is by our Viking law, was this famous fellowship founded, and by law will it be upheld."

"And is it not upheld?" asked Sigvald.

"No it is not—not as it used to be," said Beorn. "Men sleep out of the burg of nights with your leave, sometimes a whole week at a time, visiting their friends in the country round, as if a Viking ought to have any friends except his brothers in arms."

"When Palnatoki came and seized this haven and threw a wall around it," said Sigvald, "the land was waste for miles and miles. Not a man lived in marsh and wood, for this haven had been for ages the haunt and lair of all the Vikings of the Baltic side. None left the burg because in all the country round there was not a soul to be seen. But here the old saw has come to be true, 'Set a thief to catch a thief.'

Now that Jomsburg is a place of strength, both to Burislaf and ourselves, his people have built them houses, and broken up the woods and marshes into farms and homesteads. They sleep peacefully under the shadow of these walls, for what Viking band, or what King in all the North would dare to harry or lay waste those whom we shield with our arms. That, Beorn, is why we have, not broken, but relaxed the law. A leather thong may stretch and be as good as ever again, but break it and its use is gone for ever, and so it is with the law. Palnatoki suffered no one to go out of the Castle for more than three nights, for if any man was to be found near us he was an enemy ; now the land is filled with the smiling faces of our friends, to whom we sell our wheat and meal and thralls and all our fair female slaves. No harm can come of visiting those who owe so much to us.

"Break the law in one thing," said Beorn, "and you break it in all ;" and then looking sternly at Sigvald, he said, "Next we shall have women in the burg, and Captains married."

"And why not?" asked Thorkell.

"Why not," repeated Beorn ; "with that

question goes another of our laws. When we take to asking why women should not be in Jomsburg, and why Captains should not be married, I foresee the ruin of Jomsburg.

"Was not Palnatoki married himself?" asked Sigvald "and were not you married in your own country, Beorn the Welshman?"

"It is true," said Beorn, "that my foster-brother Palnatoki, our founder, was married. Here is Vagn, his lawful grandchild, to prove that, but Palnatoki had no wife when he founded Jomsburg; and as for mine, she was dead and gone in Wales, even before he and I mingled our blood, and passed under the sod of turf, and became foster-brothers. What I said before, I say still. No Viking, Captain or common man should be married. Marriage is the root of all evil in the band; and when wives come into the burg at one gate our glory will depart from us at the other."

As the old Viking was so stubborn, neither Sigvald nor Thorkell cared to stay any longer to continue the discussion, but left Vagn and Beorn to themselves.

As they parted, Sigvald said to Beorn, "You

will be in your seat in the hall this evening, messmate. I have news which I wish to share with all the Captains of the band."

"News," said Beorn. "No news is good news," says the old saw. "If it were an autumn cruise to England to harry Ethelred's land, it would be another thing; or to Norway against Earl Hacon, or even to Denmark against my old comrade Sweyn, the son of the seamstress, that would be news indeed; news such as we had in olden days; but this news, I'll bet my best broad axe, will be only some soft words from Burislaf, whose messenger, as I told you, has been in the burg, and, like a leaky pot, has already let fall the purport of his message, and that is, our Captain Sigvald thinks of breaking the law and taking to him a wife."

"Tell me, foster-brother," said Vagn, "how the vessel came to leak; how did you crack it and make it yield its liquor?"

"Not as I would have wished," said Beorn, "by giving him a knock on his shaven pate. I hate these monks, whom Burislaf sends always telling what they call their beads, always pattering their paternosters; if they sing, singing doleful strains; quite unlike Einar Scaleclang, or Gunnlaug Snaketongue. How Egill, the son Grim-Baldpate, would have laughed at their music. And then that choking stuff which they call incense"——

How much longer Beorn would have gone on in this abuse of monks, no one can tell, had not Vagn checked him by asking:

"But the message, the news, foster-father? How did you get the mead out of the flask if you did not crack it by a blow?"

"By pouring in the mead itself. That fine strong English mead which you and I got as part of our spoil when last summer we threw in our lot with Olaf Tryggvi's son, and harried Sussex, while Ethelred the unready fled before us."

"I have heard," said Vagn, "that monks drink no ale or wine. How then did Burislaf's priest drink mead?"

"You had better ask him that question when you next see him in the Captain's hall," said Beorn; "I can only tell you what he told me before he departed, 'Mead,' he said, 'was not ale, and it was not wine. Both these he was forbidden to drink, but mead he was not,' and then he sate him down and drank stoup after stoup of the rich amber drink, and the end was that it took hold of him, and he spoke, and he told me that Burislaf's message to the Captain was, that if Sigvald would come and see him, they would see whether he should have Astrida to wife."

"The Captain has a quick eye for beauty," said Vagn, "for if fame speaks truth, Astrida is by far the fairest of all King Burislaf's daughters. But Sigvald must have first asked for her hand, if Burislaf has sent that answer. Who bore the offer to the King; a bird of the air or a fish of the sea?"

"Not so," said Beorn, bitterly, "but a worm of the earth. Another of these monks whom Otho the Emperor sent to Sigvald a while ago. Don't you mind his in-coming and out-going?"

"Yes," said Vagn, "but I thought the Emperor sent him to say that it would be good for Sigvald's soul if he and all the band were turned into Christians, and forswore the old faith, if any of them still clung to it."

"True enough, boy," said Beorn, "and the Captain said he thanked the Emperor much for the care he took of the souls of the company, but that he and they trusted rather in their own good swords and stout ships and stalwart arms, than in anything else. We had most of us shaken off the fetters of the old faith, and were not so anxious to be fettered anew; and so the shaveling shook the dust off his feet, as he called it, and went on his way, telling his beads, and singing his doleful ditties; but for all that he bore a message to Burislaf, and it was that Sigvald would be willing to wed his daughter.

CHAPTER III.

THE VIKINGS IN THEIR HALL.

Now we are in the Vikings' hall, a long building, with a high pitched roof, and lighted along each side with a row of slits, too narrow for entrance, and too high to be reached very easily from the ground. At the end of each side of the building was a door, the gable ends being blank, and without door or window, and these two narrow doors were the only means of entrance or exit. Inside each door was another gate, or rather grate, through which an incomer had to make his way. After he had got so far, he turned right or left into the spacious hall. In the middle, in the winter time, blazed great fires of huge logs, the smoke from which made its way out of louvres at the top of the roof. All along the hall, on either side, ran a row of benches, and in the middle, on each side, were two high-seats, one for the Captain, and over against him that for his lieutenant, or second in command. On either side of the Captain sat the bravest and oldest of the band, their seats varying in dignity as they approached the doors on each side. This was the order on the Captain's or chief side, and the same precedence was observed on the opposite benches. The benches were not so far apart on either side that everything said or done could not be seen or heard by those who sat over against them. When meat was served, shifting tables, formed of boards supported on trestles, were borne in, and when the rude meal was over the thralls bore them away, and serious drinking, which was the business of the evening, began. Then it was that the Chief, rising in his seat, and holding out his horn of ale or mead, solemnly pledged the lieutenant opposite to him, draining the horn. The Lieutenant then rose in his turn, and pledged the Captain, whose example was followed by the Chief on his right hand, who pledged him that sate on the Lieutenant's right. Next in order came the sitter on the King's left hand, who went through the same toast with the sitter on the Lieutenant's left, and so the horn passed on, going across the hall from right to left, till every man had pledged him that sate opposite to him. It is curious that this very order of drinking healths in the loving-cup is still retained in civic feasts in England, with the addition, unknown to the earliest times, that the guests on either side of him that drinks the toast rise, as he drains the bowl, that they may guard his throat against treachery as he drinks.

As we enter the Vikings' hall, which was arranged generally in the same way as every hall royal or simple in those days, the tables have been removed, and the toasts and pledges are in progress, when the festivities are interrupted by a thrall, who played the part of master of the ceremonies, who passed up the middle of the hall and, standing before the Captain, called out in a loud voice—

"A messenger from King Burislaf."

"He is welcome," said Sigvald. "We are ready to hear his message; after that, let him have an honourable seat and drink his fill."

In strode the messenger, clad in a dark blue kirtle, red breeks, brown woollen hose, and high shoes with long laces which were wound crosswise high up the legs below the knee. In his hand he bore an axe with a long haft, not unlike the medieval halbert, and at his side he was girt with a short sword.

Bending before Sigvald he said:

"I bear a message from King Burislaf, O Captain. Wilt thou hear it now?"

"It is never too soon to listen to the words of a friend," said Sigvald; "utter your message at once, and let us all hear it."

"King Burislaf bids you welcome," said the messenger, "and asks you to come to him speedily to see him, that he may take counsel with you."

"It is well," said Sigvald. "We will consider of it and give you an answer. Meantime tell us your name, and say where you parted from the King."

"My name," said the messenger, "is Gangrel Speedifoot, and I have come hither in one day from Stargard, where I left King Burislaf in his hall."

"Speedifoot in truth," said Sigvald, "King Burislaf's messengers do not let the grass grow under their feet; forty miles and more is well run in a day. And now Beorn the Welshman make room for Gangrel Speedifoot between you and your foster-child Vagn; make him merry to-night, and see that he is not stinted in mead. To-morrow morning he shall bear our answer to King Burislaf."

Again the messenger bowed low before the Captain, and then turning away took his seat between Beorn and Vagn.

"'Tis ill jesting, they say, with a thirsty man," said the old Viking, "but I know 'tis just as ill to talk with him till he has quenched his thirst."

As he said this he held out to him a huge horn full of mantling English mead, and wished him a good errand and a safe return to King Burislaf.

Slowly the messenger raised the horn to his lips, holding it out at arm's length, and throwing back his head as he drank.

As he did this, Beorn said to Vagn:

"See how deftly he drains it without spilling a drop. 'Tis not the first time he has supped mead. See how the tail of the horn goes up and up in the air, for all the world like Thor when he tried to drink the sea dry in the Utgard's Loki."

At last the outstretched arm dropped, the horn sank slowly down, and with a deep breath followed by a grunt of satisfaction, Gangrel Speedifoot handed back the horn to Beorn, who peered into it, and said:

"Well drunk indeed, Gangrel, and never a drop left. Is that the way you Wends always drink?"

"I am no Wend," said the messenger. "If I were, my name would be 'Mystislaf,' or 'Myeckzyslaf,' or some other 'laf.' No! I come from the Low Countries between the Waal and Rhine, and as I have just drunk we all drink there."

"I might have known that," said Beorn, "by your name, which means a wanderer, and which, here in the North, we should call 'Gangrad' or 'Gangler.' The first Gangrel was the great god Odin, whom all the North used to believe in. Many is the story which tells how he walked over this middle-earth shrouded in a loose cloak and a broad flapping hat to search into the ways of men. And you, too, have seen much in your time and passed on your speedy feet through many lands."

"Have you any more of that rare English mead?" asked Gangrel with a chuckle. "How it takes hold of a man. My feet already feel it. Let me drain another horn, and then I will tell you whence I came and whither I have been."

"I have always heard that you Flemings were great drinkers," said Beorn, "and at home in Wales there are some of us mighty over the mead and the ale-horn; but your horn holds good measure, and if you drained it all to your own share you might not be able to tell your story. Besides, our way of drinking is to drink half and half with one's neighbour. See the horn is cut in half inside by a peg. Half belongs to thee and half to me." Then calling out to one of the thralls, "here lad, fill up the horn again with English mead and bear it to Gangrel Speedifoot the King's messenger."

The horn was brought, when Beorn took it and said:

"I will teach thee how to drink in Viking wise."

Then he slowly raised the tail of the horn in

air as Gangrel had done; but when it was half up he suddenly checked his hand and threw down the horn with a sudden jerk, which made the mead foam half way down the horn, but without spilling a drop.

"There!" said Beorn; "that's how we drink. But maybe you will think it not worth while to drain the little drop that is left, though it is at least a quart after our measure."

"Two things I have learned on my travels," said the messenger, "one, to be content with the half when I cannot get the whole; the other, to do as the folk do with whom I happen to be. At home we should think it a scurvy thing to drink half a horn of mead. Our horns are always filled to the brim, and we drain them to the last drop. Here you pledge each other half and half, and it is not a bad custom if one gets halves enough to make up many wholes. But I have been worse off than this, for when I was in Byzance, which you Northmen call Mickle-garth, the town of towns, I have been with folk who never touched one drop of wine or ale or mead, and yet said they did very well without them."

"And what, then, did they drink at their feasts and over the fire at Yule," asked Beorn.

"In those lands," said Gangrel Speedifoot, "there is no Yule and no fires, and what that folk drink is what we never see at our feasts—either here or in Flanders—water."

"Water," groaned out Beorn; "water! Here, boy, fill up this horn again with mead. Gangrel Speedifoot, say that over again! Travellers like you see many strange things and tell many strange stories; but who ever heard of water at a feast?"

"It is as I said," said Gangrel; "believe it or not, as you choose. When I was among the Varangians, in the Great Emperor's service, we went east to a land between two mighty rivers, and there the folk believed in a prophet, and drank no wine or ale or mead; and if one went into their tents and asked for a drink they gave you water in an earthen vessel."

"It is many years," said Beorn, sententiously, "since I had a drop of water in my mouth, except it was river-water or sea-water when a wave broke over my ship, and then, so help me both Odin and the white Christian God, and all the gods of all the creeds, I always spat it out again. How can these folk fight or sing or live at all if their blood is not stirred by ale or mead ?"

"They not only sing and live and fight," said Gangrel, "but they do all three well. Many and many of your Northern Varangians have bitten the dust after a flight of their bitter arrows. Never saw I such bowmen as those water-drinkers, or such lithe sinewy men."

"And all on water," muttered Beorn. "Well! well! the water in those lands must be stronger than the rivers and streams in these northern lands. Maybe the sun shining on it all the year round puts life and spirit into it. But not here —not in Wales nor in Flanders could men live on water alone."

"The birds and beasts and fish and monks do," said Gangrel.

"Ay! ay!" said Beorn, "but man, a real man, I mean, is, thank all the gods, not a bird or a beast or a fish or a monk. That's just what I say. What does a man live for but to fight? When he dies, our old faith says, he will go on fighting all day, and feasting and drinking in

Valhalla for ever at night. Monks do not fight, they pray both here and hereafter, but a real man must drink strong drink. Now, lad! why so slow in filling up that horn?"

The horn came, the old toper drank his share, and Gangrel finished it with a smack of his lips.

"Now, Beorn," he said, "I have told you of the land where there is no Yule and no snow, and where the folk live and fight well on naught but water. You drain your horn like a man, but you have done much beside drink in your life."

"Why ask for an old story?" broke in Vagn, who up to this time had sat still and listened. "All the world knows that for forty years at least Beorn the Welshman has fed the ravens, the yellow-footed kites, and the grey wolves."

"True as steel, I daresay," said Gangrel Speedifoot; "that is, true of all the northern world, but the world has other parts, and for many years I have been away from it, and have not heard of Beorn's brave deeds."

"Would you like another half horn?" asked Beorn. "I find it helps the memory. Perhaps, then, I might tell you one bit of my life. Not out of boasting, but as something in which I shared, though the chief glory was with my foster-brother, Palnatoki, the founder of this gallant company."

"'Tis never too late or too early for good drink," said Gangrel; "though I have been among the water-drinkers and did as they did, because I could not help it, I am ever ready for a horn of stinging ale or mead, and it is all the better if it clears the throat for a good story which deserves to live for ever. So up with the horn and out with the story; the night is still young, and the fires blaze fiercely, and all round the hall runs wassail and song, man pledging man, and cheering his neighbour. Yes, yes, by all the gods, save those of the water-drinkers, another horn of mead!"

The mead came and was soon despatched. Then Beorn cleared his throat, and said:

"You have heard of King Harold Bluetooth, the father of King Sweyn, the son of the seamstress, the King of Denmark that now is?"

"I have heard of him in my youth, before I left your land for the East," said Gangrel; "but what he did and how he died is more than I can tell."

"Then hear how he died and how we drank his funeral ale; as for his life, he was a bad, unjust king, and the less said of him the better. At the end of his days he had one son left, Sweyn, the son of the seamstress, whom Palnatoki fostered and brought up. It so happened that King Harold would never own him to be his son, though all the world knew it as plain as day, and the end of it was that from words that father and son fell to blows, and Palnatoki of course sided with his foster-child. It also happened that Palnatoki had to go west one summer to see after a little kingdom which he had won in Wales. There it was that I became his foster-brother; but of that I will say naught. While Palnatoki was away, King Harold got the better of his son, and at last caught him in a cleft stick, that is, he shut him up with his ships in an inlet like this of ours before we built the castle; and more than that, he was strong enough to land with a band of his men on either side of the inlet while his ships lay in a double line across the haven's mouth. Do you carry it in your head, or is the mead too strong for you?"

"I carry it all in my head just as well as I carry the mead," was the reply.

"Very well," said Beorn. "Then I go on to say that on the very night that all this happened, Sweyn's good luck, or the will of the gods, brought Palnatoki back from Wales, and we pulled up in the dark to a little bay not a mile from where the two fleets lay. Though they knew nothing of us, we had heard from some fishermen in the Sound that the King and Sweyn were at loggerheads on the Swedish shore. So being forewarned we were forearmed, and Palnatoki soon found out that Sweyn was hemmed in, and that between him and his foster-child lay King Harold and his force.

"As soon as our ship was safely moored, he said to me, 'Foster-brother, hast thou a mind to land with me to see how the land lies. If Sweyn is to be saved at all, he must be saved to-night. To-morrow it will be too late!'

"'How he is to be saved to-night, when it is

too dark to fight, I cannot see,' I said; 'but if you like, we will land.'

"So we landed, taking with us our axes and shields, and Palnatoki, who was the best bowman in the North, worth a hundred of your water-drinkers, had his bow and arrows. Well, we had not gone more than a mile across the wooded hill that skirted the shore, when we saw among the trees a great fire of logs, and men standing and sitting round it, for it was already past the first winter-night, and the weather was cold.

"'These be some of the King's men, foster-brother,' said Palnatoki; 'let us go closer to them.'

"So we crept up to them among the trees. It was an easy task; they could not see us, but they stood out clear to us before the fire, and as for hearing us, the wind blew and the flames crackled and roared so that we could have stolen close up to them unawares. But we had no need to do so. When we were half a bow-shot, it may be, off, my foster-brother whispered to me:

"'This is a royal hunt indeed! It is the King himself!'

"Yes! it was the King: there he stood, with a steel cap on his head, round which was a fillet of gold, and a-top of it a golden boar; and just then he turned his face towards us, lifted up the lappets of his mantle, and warmed himself over the blazing logs.

"'This is how I save Sweyn,' said Palnatoki, as he fitted an arrow to his bowstring. In another moment loud sang the string as the arrow sped on its way, and in another down fell King Harold, stricken dead by the great marksman. There among the blazing logs he lay sprawling, while his chiefs swarmed round him; but it was all no good. King Harold Bluetooth lay dead, slain by an arrow, and none could tell who had launched the shaft.

"As for us, we two turned and went back to our ships.

"'I knew,' said Palnatoki, 'that something was in the wind, my nose itched so as we went along. But not a word, foster-brother, of this to any one. Sweyn is saved. I will send word to-night to him to try to break out of the inlet to-morrow morning at early dawn, while we row up and attack the King's men in the rear. Then it will be they, and not Sweyn, who will find themselves in a cleft stick, and we will not let them out of it until the whole host has acknowledged my foster-child as lawful King of Denmark.'

"To make a long story short," said Beorn, "the King's host were thrown into confusion and dismay by his sudden death, and next morning, with little or no bloodshed, Denmark had a young king, the King Sweyn that now is, instead of the old King Harold Bluetooth. That is the first fitte of my story, and if you wish to hear the rest, say the word and we'll drain another horn of mead before we finish it."

"With all my heart," said Gangrel Speedifoot; "I like the story almost as well as I like the mead."

"Ho! boy!" bawled Beorn, "another horn of mead for King Burislaf's messenger."

CHAPTER IV.

KING HAROLD'S BURIAL ALE.

After that last horn Beorn took breath and went on.

"As soon as Sweyn was firmly set up as King, Palnatoki went back to his kingdom in Wales, and left his son, this Vagn's father here, to manage his estates in Denmark, which he had got back with the new King. I do not know how it is with you in Flanders, Gangrel, but here in the North no man, from the King on the throne to the lowest freeman in his cottage, is thought to have entered fully on his rights, and to have done his sacred duty by the dead till he has drunk what we call his heir of heirship, or funeral ale, and held a high feast in his father's hall in honour of his memory."

"We have no such custom in Flanders," said Gangrel; "but there we are always drinking ale in our own honour. In this respect a father's death makes no difference; the son takes his land and goods, and drinks ale and mead just as before."

"Not so with us," said Beorn. "It makes no odds with us whether a father and son have been at daggers drawn when they were alive; if within three years the son has not drunk his ale of heirship, he is looked on as a 'niddering' and a dastard, and no true son of his father. Now, as I have told you, there was no love lost between that father and son. Harold would have slain Sweyn, and Sweyn Harold; but when Harold was dead, Sweyn could not be his lawful heir till he had held that feast. That is one of our customs; and we have another too, which no doubt you also have, for it runs all the world over. I daresay your water-drinkers have it too. This is what we call the blood-feud, and by it Sweyn was bound to avenge his father's death on the man who had slain him."

"We have that custom," said the Fleming, "and the water-drinkers have it too. But if Sweyn owed so much to Palnatoki, and was his foster-child as well, perhaps he might have taken an atonement."

"You neither know our customs nor Sweyn's nature," said Beorn; "but hear my story out. All this time, you must know, not a soul but Palnatoki and I knew that it was Palnatoki's arrow that had slain the King; at least, we thought no one knew it. But for all that, when Palnatoki was safe away west in Wales he did not seem so eager to return to Denmark to be present at that funeral ale. Three times in three following years did King Sweyn send and bid him to the feast, and once did Palnatoki say that he was ill, and could not come, and once that his father-in-law had died, and therefore he could not come. As the King could not, or would not, hold the feast without his foster-father, he put it off twice; but he was angry at it, and so, when the third year came, he sent so hot a message that Palnatoki made up his mind to go, and said he would not fail to be in the King's hall at Slesvig by a certain day in autumn. Well, as I said before, to make a long story short, we launched three brave ships, manned by one hundred men, and though the way was long and the weather bad, we reached our haven the very day that the feast was to be held. Whether it were chance, or whether this was Palnatoki's purpose I cannot say, but so it was; we did not reach the Slei till it was well-nigh dark. Then we laid up our ships close to the shore in deep water, and we turned their prows out to the sea, and we laid the oars ready in the rowlocks, and we left a man or two to mind them. Some of us thought all this odd, but I did not, for I was in the secret and knew what was passing in my foster-brother's mind. All the rest obeyed and said nothing, as true sailors ought.

"Well, our haven was close to the King's hall, but it was so near a thing, that when we got into the hall the King and his men were all hard at drink; still so sure was he that we would come that he had kept seats on the bench over against him for one hundred men. Right glad was he to see us, and many were the greetings that passed between him and his foster-father. So there we sat and drank and were merry, and never had there been such an ale of heirship in Denmark before, no, not even for Gorm the Old, when he and Queen Thyra died. But it was not to end well, for you must know that Palnatoki had a brother named Feolner, who had ever been against him, and who had been King Harold's counsellor. There was no love lost between him and Palnatoki, and we all thought it a bad sign when we saw that he was in high favour with King Sweyn, and sat next him at the feast.

"At last, just when the mirth and revelry were at their height, and the ale and mead began to speak in men, Feolner leant back and said something in the King's ear, and all at once he grew as red as blood, and seemed to swell all over with rage. Then up rose a man, one of the King's candlebearers, and stood before the King, and Feolner handed him an arrow on which a golden thread was twisted in the feathering, and said out loud, so that all could hear—

"'Bear this arrow round the hall, and ask every man if he knows it again and owns to it.'

"So round the hall went Arnmod—that was the candlebearer's name—all along the benches on the King's side, asking each man if he knew the arrow, and none owned it. Then he crossed the hall and came over to our side of the hall, where our men sate on the outer bench, but none owned it; and at last he came to Palnatoki in his turn.

"'Knowest thou this arrow?' he said, as he stood before him.

"'Why should I not know my own shaft?' answers Palnatoki. 'Hand it over, for it belongs to me.'

"All this while there was dead silence in the hall, for men were all listening to hear if any man would own the arrow.

"But as soon as the King heard what Palnatoki said, he called out—

"'Palnatoki, where was it that thou partedst from this arrow last?'

"'Often have I done your bidding, foster-child mine,' answered Palnatoki; 'and now, if you think your glory will be any the greater by my answering outright before all this great company rather than before a few, still I am ready to do your bidding. Know then, O King! that I parted with it from my bowstring when I shot your father, King Harold; so that my shaft went in at his midrif and came out at his mouth.'

"'Up, men!' roared out the King; 'up, and seize Palnatoki and his comrades, and slay them all, for now there is an end of all friendship between me and Palnatoki, and of all the love that was between us.'

"At this there was a hum of voices and a crash of arms throughout the hall, and men sprung up on all sides of us, and up we rose too, as you may trow, with our arms in our hands; but Palnatoki was the readiest of all of us, for in a trice he had his sword drawn, and made a dash at his kinsman Feolner and cleft him at one stroke down to the chine. But even then he had many old friends in the hall, and Feolner few, and none bore weapon on us as we made for the hall-door, all of us except one Welshman of our band; for we were half Northmen and half from Wales. When we got out safe and sound we found he was missing."

Here Beorn made a pause, as though he would have stopped; but Vagn said to Gangrel, "Make him tell his tale out; there is more to come."

"Tell on," said the Fleming.

"Well, if a man must praise himself he must," said Beorn. "Know then, that when we got out, and missed our Welshman, Palnatoki said such a loss was to be looked for, and it was no use going back to seek for him, and was all for going down at once to our ships, but I withstood him, and said:

"'Thou wouldst not run so from one of thine own men, nor will I.' And so I turned back into the hall to look for him; but when I got inside there they were tossing him about on the points of their spears, and had almost torn him to pieces; but by good luck I got hold of him and flung him over my back and ran out with him and the King's men after me, and then we all rushed down to the ships."

"Bravely done indeed," said Gangrel; "but was he quite dead?"

"Dead as Balder," said Beorn, "after the mistletoe went through him, or as Harold after Palnatoki's shaft. But I bore his body down to the shore, and then we got on shipboard and fell to our oars long before Sweyn's men could launch a ship. It was pitch dark, but the sea was smooth as glass, and so our three war-snakes cut the waters, and in much less time than we had taken to come we were safe back in Wales. And that was how Palnatoki owned his arrow, and how King Sweyn kept his father's funeral ale."

"And how you stood by your Welshman and carried him off; all these are feats which will be told and talked of in the North so long as the world lasts."

"I do not know that," said the old Viking; "but that's how those things happened, and that's how the blood-feud arose between King Sweyn and Palnatoki."

"It was after that he built Jomsburg; this castle that we are now in?" asked the Fleming.

"It was," said Beorn. "You see in some things Palnatoki was the unluckiest of men. So long as King Harold was alive he was an outlaw, because he stood by Sweyn, the seamstress's son, and after he had raised Sweyn to the throne by that happy shot, in stepped the blood-feud, and made him just as great an outlaw to Harold's son. But in one thing Sweyn was good; he did not confiscate Palnatoki's goods in Fünen, but let Aki Vagn's father have the keeping of them, and they will belong some day or other to my foster-child, just as Strut-Harold's earldom in Scania will belong one fine day to our captain Sigvald, and Bornholm will belong to Bui the Stout yonder when the gods take his father Veseti to themselves."

"Why, you are all elder sons," said Gangrel, "waiting, like Sweyn, to drink his own father's funeral ale. But you, at least, Beorn, are too old to have a father alive. You must long ago have come into your inheritance. How fares it with your kingdom in the West?"

"Much as it fares with all the kingdoms of the West," said Beorn; "one day smiling, one day waste. As for me, I left my lands to my kinsmen when I threw in my lot with Palnatoki and came here. Some day or other I may return, but as yet I have never been homesick; and besides, Palnatoki on his deathbed left me his grandchild Vagn to take care of. He is already equal to any of our band, but the day will come when no one in the North will dare to stand before him."

"But see, Gangrel," he went on, "the fires

burn low, the captain rises, and Bui and Thorkell follow his example. There is but time for one more horn of mead before we lie down to sleep. Boy! boy! another horn for Gangrel Speedifoot. Dear me, how dry telling these long stories makes a man feel in the throat."

"Could you drink water now if you were with the water-drinkers?" said Gangrel.

"I will wait till I get to their country," answered Beorn; "till then I will make shift to stay my thirst with English mead."

Then the pair drained their last horn, and followed the rest of the Vikings out of the hall to the log cabins, in which they slept by twos and threes.

As Sigvald left the hall he said to Gangrel Speedifoot:

"To-morrow at the morning meal, when the sun has risen as high as half the shaft of this spear above the Griffonberg yonder, you shall have our answer to King Burislaf."

CHAPTER V.

THE ANSWER TO KING BURISLAF AND WHAT CAME OF IT.

THOUGH not very early in going to bed, the Vikings were early risers. In the summer they rose hours before they had their breakfast, and evidently had no rules as to the harm of fasting and working on an empty stomach. At the particular time of the year of which we write—September—they rose at five, but they had no food till nine, and it was just at that time that the sun was half the height of Sigvald's spear above the low hill called the Griffonberg, as he held it straight before him at arm's length and measured the sun's lower limb by a rude sort of trigonometry.

There were but two meals in the day in those times in the North—day-meal, or breakfast, and night-meal, or supper; the first at nine a.m. and the other at the same hour at night, so that there were about twelve hours between each. Of these, more was eaten at breakfast and more drunk at supper. The porridge and joints were heavy at both, and ale and mead flowed without stint; but still, as we have said, much more was eaten at the first, and after draining a horn or two men went about their business and their work, while at supper work was over for the day, and the band sat drinking over the fires, as we have said, till far on in the night.

At breakfast, therefore, on that September morning, Gangrel Speedifoot again met Sigvald, and again was handed over to the care of his messmate Beorn.

"Well, Gangrel, hast thou slept sound after that stinging English mead? It was all needed to wash down Beorn's long stories. And your appetite, has it failed you, or wilt thou try your teeth on this wild boar?"

"I have slept well," answered Gangrel. "The mead did not rob me of my rest, and Beorn's stories, though long, were some of the best I have ever heard."

"Ah!" said Sigvald, "they are fresh to you; you have never heard them before."

"Deeds like those of Palnatoki are ever fresh," said Gangrel. "You will have hard work to achieve greater things."

"Say you so," cried Sigvald. "Well, well, Palnatoki was a gallant captain, but perhaps ere we bite the dust I and my brother Thorkell, and Bui, and Vagn, and even old Beorn himself, may do something which shall even eclipse his fame."

"Would that it might be so," said the messenger; "but the sun is already more than half shaft high. I have eaten my fill, the way is long, the day short, and I shall have to run more swiftly than I ran yesterday if I am to reach Stargard to-night. What is your answer to King Burislaf, my master?"

"Tell your master," said the captain, "that three nights from this I will sup with him in his hall at Stargard with fifty of my men."

"A good message makes a merry messenger," said Gangrel Speedifoot, with a bow to Sigvald. "Thanks for making my errand hither lucky. Thanks to thee, Beorn, and to thee, Vagn, and thanks, last of all, to this gallant company.

Jomsburg lacks naught that I can see save the presence of women."

"Perhaps we may mend that want even yet," said Sigvald, as Gangrel Speedifoot passed out of the hall, and was soon beyond the walls on his way to King Burislaf.

Though none of the band, save Beorn, had got an inkling of what Burislaf's message meant, and even he had only half guessed the truth, Sigvald and his brother well knew its purport. It was quite true, as Beorn had said, that Sigvald was sick of a single life, and as true that he had turned his eyes on one of King Burislaf's daughters. That he was in love with a woman whom he had never seen was as little likely in that age as this. There had been cases in Northern tradition like that in which a great king had given up his heart at once to a maiden one of whose long golden hairs had been dropped by a raven at his feet, but these were exceptions. Sigvald, the son and heir of the proud Earl Strut-Harold, of Scania, was eager to marry, that he might have an heir to succeed him. He had not thought of this when, like so many of the leaders of the band, he had sailed with his ships to join the Vikings, and when he had accepted the captainship, and sworn to obey the laws, which in this point, at least, he was now ready to break. The priest of whom Beorn had spoken had sounded Burislaf on the matter, and the mission of Gangrel Speedifoot was the result. We have heard what the King's messenger said. He was willing to see Sigvald with a strong escort in his grange near Stargard, but he had said nothing of the proposed marriage. This exactly suited Sigvald's views, for he could not take a wife without the leave of the band, and that leave he must get before he started on his wooing.

"So to-morrow there is to be a muster in full arms in the open field," said Beorn to Vagn. "We must all be there. Depend on it the Captain has something to say about this visit to the King."

"By this time to-morrow," answered Vagn, "we shall know all about it. Meantime, what is the use of guessing what it may be?"

"Take my word for it, it will be about breaking the law and taking a wife," said Beorn.

"Well, then," said Vagn, "I for one shall vote for it."

"You vote for it, foster-child; you! such a boy as you are!"

"Who knows," said Vagn, "if the law is changed whether I may not carry off and wed Thorkell of Leira's daughter, Ingibeorg the fair."

"Sets the wind in that quarter still?" said Beorn, with a grunt. "We are all going down hill as fast as we can."

To-morrow came, and with it the grand muster of the Vikings on the plain outside the walls where so many combats had been fought by candidates for admission to the band. As the Vikings filed through the narrow gate of the burg a mere glance at them would have shown why this famous company were the terror of the North. Taking the crews of their three hundred ships at the very lowest estimate, they must have numbered ten thousand, made up of the squadrons which great chiefs such as Sigvald, Beorn, Thorkell, Bui, and Vagn had brought with them. Even under such leaders, all, as we have seen, were not indiscriminately admitted. None of the rank and file were beyond the limits of age, and none passed muster for entrance who was not a picked man. A modern observer would have called them, when considered as sailors, all A.B.'s, and as soldiers all grenadiers. On and on they passed on that September morning through the gate, armed with axe and sword and spear and bow, but, as we have said before, with no defensive armour except a shield. Those were not the days of uniforms, and yet in a certain sense all the Vikings of less mark wore a garb more or less alike—a kirtle, breeks, and hose of coarse russet woollen, shoes of brown tanned leather, and on their heads a low-crowned hat, the ancestor of our modern wide-awake. A few among the ranks wore a steel hat, and a "byrnie" or shirt of linked mail; but these were so rare as to be scarcely worth notice. Slowly the whole body, marching as one man, with a tramp that made the peaty soil shake, formed themselves into a hollow square, within which stood Sigvald and his chiefs.

In the midst of the square was an ancient cairn of huge stones, the last resting-place, before it had been ransacked by the Vikings, of some Wendish chief. It was, in fact, precisely what is called a cromlech in Wales—that is, the cist or sepulchral chamber of a barrow, denuded of the earth and gravel which had been piled over it to form the tomb. There on the top of the horizontal slab the Viking Captains had always stood when they wished to address the band ; but to the surprise of all, instead of Sigvald, Thorkell now took his place, and began to speak in what the chronicler of that day calls "a clever oration."

"Vikings of Jomsburg," he said, "we have met here to-day that I may tell you something which concerns us all. You know all of you how long this company has lasted, and won fame and fee by the wise laws which our old captain Palnatoki framed. These laws have made us what we are, and by them we mean to abide."

Here there was a hum of applause and a crash of arms as each man smote the iron boss of his shield with his sword. As the sound died away Thorkell went on—

"We mean to abide in them, I say, so far as we can ; but laws grow old like all things else on this middle-earth, and what is easy to one man to bear is a heavy burden to another. Palnatoki was an old man when he came hither with Beorn the Welshman, whom we all know and all admire as one of our boldest. He had already done with wife and child. The oak had shed its apple on the earth, and borne goodly saplings like his grandson Vagn here, the bravest and strongest for his years of all our company. One head of our laws, therefore, which many of us find very hard to bear, was light as a feather to Palnatoki. To him the love of woman was a thing past and gone. In that he had quenched his thirst, and drained his horn to the dregs. But it is not so with most of us. How many of you are like Freyr the ancient god, in whom some of us still believe, when he saw Gerda in the grange of Gymir the giant, and was so devoured by love of her that unless he had gotten her to wife he had died? How many of us, as we have dashed in our sea-stags through the billows of the West, on landing have found among the spoil lovely maidens of high birth, and felt like Freyr, but, unlike the god, have known that we were cut off from them except

as slaves to sell by laws made by (
selves."

Here another murmur of applause show
that in that assemblage of youth and vigo
there were many who acknowledged the trut
of Thorkell's words.

"I think, therefore," Thorkell went on, "tha
this law as to bringing women and wives into
the burg, and as to marriage, might be changed;
not all at once, but that some of us might, with
the Captain's leave and the leave of the company,
have power to take a wife. It is a wise saying
of our forefathers which bids us beware of too
much of a good thing. Thousands, or even
hundreds, of women in Jomsburg might ruin our
company, but ten or fifty would not. No doubt
the Captain has often felt like Freyr, and longed
for an heir to that earldom in Denmark which
our father Strut-Harold holds. He is a gallant
captain, and Jomsburg holds her head as high
under him as she did in the days of Palnatoki.
But we can do nothing without the laws of the
band, and so I ask you to vote that the law
may be eased on this one point, and that the
Captain may have leave to marry and bring his

wife home, and that he may, if he sees fit, allow any of you who does a deed of 'derring do' to take a wife to himself and bring her home if he pleases. And now, before you vote, we are ready to hear what any man has to say for or against the marriage of the Captain."

As the tall Viking jumped down from the slab on one side, it was slowly mounted on the other by Beorn the Welshman.

"I am no speaker, like Thorkell Glibtongue, as I call him, rather than the Tall ; and the Captain, if he wishes the law to be broken, has done well to put his brother forward, who can say things for the Captain which he could not say for himself. It is fine talking to say that the Captain is like Freyr, and longs for a wife like Gerda of the white arms, but Thorkell forgets the price which Freyr paid for Gerda, and how he had to give up that good sword to the giant which would stand him in good stead at the great day of doom, the Twilight of the Gods. That price was too great when weighed against the white arms of Gerda, and so this company will pay too great a price if women and wives come into the burg, in the ruin that will surely come as soon as the old laws are broken. It is all very well to talk of tens or fifties of women. We have all seen how thin a wedge will rend asunder an oaken trunk ; so it will be with us. To my mind one woman is as bad as a thousand. We get on very well as we are without them ; why not let well alone."

At this telling speech of the old Welshman, there was again a murmur of applause in the ranks, but it was not so loud as that which followed Thorkell's speech. Some shouts were heard too of "the Captain, the Captain ; let him speak, let him speak."

Then Sigvald mounted the slab, and there arose a roar of voices, and another mighty crash of arms, as every man smote his shield with redoubled force.

"I am not so good at speech as my brother Thorkell," he said, "who can do all things well—sail a ship, smite a foe, sing a song, or make a speech. And, though Beorn would have you believe that he is no speaker, you have heard what he said and how well he spoke it. As for me, it is true, as my brother said, that I wish to marry, that Strut-Harold's enemies may not believe that his race will die out because his two sons have thrown in their lot with you, and are bound by the laws not to take to themselves a wife. I am not like Freyr, for I have not yet seen my Gerda, and I am not pining myself to death, like Freyr, for her sake. I own, though, that I have turned my eyes where I know good women are to be found, and that is to King Burislaf's grange; but I know not till I see these fair maidens whether I shall love them as Freyr did Gerda. But this, at least, I know, that not for the sake of any woman will I, like Freyr, give up this my good sword, which has cloven so many of the foes of this gallant company to the chine."

At this utterance there was another roar of voices, and another crash of arms, and Sigvald went on.

"There is another thing which the company should think over, and that is, though I am loath to say it, that times and seasons and men change. My father, Strut-Harold, is an old man, and before he dies I should wish that he saw an heir to his earldom in a son of mine. Were he to die, and I be still unwedded, I should give up the captainship and leave the burg, that I might drink my father's funeral ale and marry. But if the law were changed as to marriage, I should stay here and still be Captain, and Thorkell, one of the mainstays of the band, would stay with me; but if the law abides as it is, in a little time we must both go."

It was easy to see that this too was an arrow that went home. There was no one in the band who, for birth and bearing, could compare with Sigvald. Bui and Vagn, and his brother Thorkell, might be stronger and more daring in fight, but Sigvald, besides a strong arm, had a good head on his shoulders, and this the band well knew, and even Beorn, his great antagonist, had to confess it. If Sigvald went, it was as though the wit and wisdom of the company departed with him. This was clearly shown when the next speaker arose to address the crowd.

"My name is Bui, as you all know, son of Veseti of Bornholm. My words are really few, and this is what I say. Women and marriage in the burg are an evil and a curse, but it would be worse far to lose Sigvald. It would be as the gods found out when Odin was lost from

Asgard, and Thor had the rule in his own hands. I shall never marry ; my good ship and my two chests full of golden spoil are treasures enough for me. But what is one man's poison is another's meat, and sooner than lose Sigvald and Thorkell, let us give them leave to marry Hela herself if they please."

This short speech from one of the opposition party, as Bui might be justly called, settled the question. Thorkell, who knew the advantage of striking while the iron was hot, sprang upon the slab and roared out, in words which reached every man of the company, "How say ye, Vikings of Jomsburg, shall Sigvald, our captain, have leave to marry and to allow others to marry at his own choice ; yes or no ?"

"Yes ! yes !" roared the mighty crowd, now completely moved and magnetized. "Yes ! yes ! let him marry as he pleases." And so, with another great crash of arms, that question, in which Beorn saw the ruin of the company, was carried by acclamation.

CHAPTER VI.

KING BURISLAF AND HIS DAUGHTERS.

Now the story goes to the grange of King Burislaf, which lay some way outside the town of Stargard. The kings of that race, though the Wends dwelt much in towns, followed the fashion of the German tribes, and lived for the most part in the open country, shunning walls in which they could be cooped up like mice, and preferring to hear the birds sing, and to see the green grass grow and the tall trees bud and bloom. This grange of King Burislaf was not at all palatial. It had an ample hall, which stood apart by itself, in which the King sat every day and drank and feasted with about a hundred retainers of his body-guard. One reason why he was anxious to be on good terms with the Vikings was, that listening to the exhortations of the Emperor Otho's priests, he had become half, if not entirely a Christian. He had been what the Northmen called "signed with the cross," or "primsigned," traces of which practice linger still in the English baptismal service in the words, "and do sign him with the sign of the cross." It was the first step to baptism, but not baptism itself, and those who had received it were admitted to social life with Christians, and to a portion of their mass. If they died they were buried on the outskirts of the churchyards where consecrated and unconsecrated earth met; but the service of the church was not read over them. While he was in this half and half state of religious belief, which well represented the shifting character of the time, his subjects, the Wends, were for the most part obstinate heathen, and if they could have combined against Burislaf, would have burnt him and sacrificed him to their idols; but so long as harvests were good and the King's Christianity was kept in the background, the Wends still yielded him a surly obedience, partly for the sake of his descent from the old royal race and partly from fear lest the Emperor Otho should treat them as he had treated the heathen kingdom of Denmark in Harold Bluetooth's time, and convert them to Christianity by a German crusade waged with fire and sword.

Besides the hall the King's grange consisted of a series of separate buildings forming four sides of a square, in the centre of which the hall itself stood. One of these was a kitchen, another stables for horses and kine, over which was a long loft in which the King's body-guard slept. Another was the Queen's parlour, another the King's treasury and counting-house, in which he certainly counted out his money when he had any, though it is doubtful whether the Queen ever ate bread and honey in her own apartment. Another was the ladies' bower, and it is into this that we now usher the reader and introduce him at once to King Burislaf, his queen, and his three daughters.

The King was a short, oily-looking man, with a sleek, sly expression of face. The kings of those days just as little as kings in modern times, were in the habit of wearing their state clothes on all occasions. Burislaf was, therefore, dressed pretty much like any other Wend of rank, in woollen outer garments of finer quality, though under his kirtle, instead of linen, he wore a silken shirt, which had come across Russia from Byzantium. Round his brow he wore a circlet of gold as a token of his rank, and in like manner the Queen and the Princesses wore thin fillets of the same metal.

In these days we fancy that the costume called "Bloomer" is a modern invention, but in reality it was but a revival of the women's dress in the early ages. Their under-clothing was of fine linen, a smock fitting close up to the throat, over that they wore a woollen skirt or petticoat, which came down just below the knee, under that their extremities were clothed in full drawers or trousers coming down to the ankle. These, with a kirtle or long jacket, woollen stockings, and high shoes, made up the women's attire of the tenth century. Over all, especially when out of doors, both men and women wore a cloak, and in the family of Burislaf silk seemed so common that all these fair members of the royal family wore kirtles of silk.

We have already described King Burislaf. If he upheld his ascendancy at home and respect abroad, it was not by the strength of his arm, but by the goodness of his head. He was wily and politic above the princes of the time, and he had been taught this policy by the continued struggles he had to keep on good terms with the Emperor, to save appearances with his heathen people, to keep the Vikings in good humour, and, in a word, to make both ends meet when both ends were far too short.

The Queen had been a lovely Princess of the Russian race, which then ruled at Novgorod and on the Ladoga, and played so large a part in the history of the time. She had been tall and fair, as well as proud and haughty, but twenty-five years of married life with Burislaf had played sad havoc with her looks as well as with her pride. She was very different from the dainty princess who had once refused prince after prince who came a-wooing to Novgorod, and all for what? To marry Burislaf, whose lineage went up straight to the Wendish gods, but who at last, to add to his other troubles, had been reduced to promise to pay tribute to the King of Denmark. These humiliations, and the possibility, we might even add the probability, that the fanatical Wendish priests might raise a levy of heathens and burn

King Burislaf and the Queen and the Princesses in one of their granges, added an excitement not attended with dignity to the Queen's existence.

But the Princesses! Yes, they were Princesses indeed—lovely young things, full of life and strength—except one very unlike Burislaf, and very like their mother. That was the way in which the natural pride of the Queen had revenged itself on her husband. She had no son, but two of her daughters were as little like Burislaf as the Queen was like him.

Their names! these Princesses. Astrida was the eldest, and wisest, and fairest. Gunnhilda was the second, less wise and most like her father; and last of all came Geira, the least fair and leastwise of them. The reader need not trouble himself with her, as she is out of the story—she married King Olaf, the son of Tryggvi, and may be heard of in his Saga.

Just as we enter that bower of the Wendish royal family, it is plain that all things have not been very smooth. It may help us to understand the matter if we say that outside, just in the very act of leaving the royal presence, we meet

Gangrel Speedifoot, who, having run all the way from Jomsburg, and having arrived late in the night when King Burislaf was snoring off his carouse, had delayed delivering his message till the next morning. So that it happened that at the very time that the Vikings were debating at their muster whether the Captain should be allowed to marry, King Burislaf and his wife and daughters were discussing Sigvald, and what answer should be given to him when he came in two days to ask for the hand of one of the Princesses.

What the Queen had said we know not. Something no doubt to the effect that Burislaf had better put the Captain off, for Burislaf in answer said :—

"But suppose he will not be put off? Suppose Sigvald gives up the captainship, as Gangrel Speedifoot believes he will, and the company breaks up, where should we be without the safeguard which the Vikings are to us against foemen from the sea. All these fair fields would be ravaged, and we should lose untold sums."

"But how do you know he will choose any one of us?" said Gunnhilda. "He may not like us when he sees us."

"That," said Burislaf, "has never happened in our family. One of you he will choose, and that one will not be you, Gunnhilda, but Astrida."

"She is eldest and wisest, and ought to be chosen first," said Gunnhilda, rather glad at the prospect of getting rid of a suitor she had never seen.

"Indeed!" said Astrida, "it ill suits my temper or my rank to be so given away. Now do you think, father, that Sigvald is a fit mate to one of our royal race."

"His father, Strut-Harold, the earl, thinks no small things of himself," said Burislaf; "and by all accounts Sigvald is equal to his father, at least in his own conceit."

"Deep-witted you are said to be, father," said Astrida, "think of some plan by which you may get rid of Sigvald as a suitor, and yet keep him in good humour."

"Spoken after my own heart," said Burislaf. "I am quite content if that can only be done. But if I am deep-witted, so are you, Astrida, and besides you have quite as much at stake in this as I. If Sigvald comes with fifty men at his back, and his choice falls on you, what answer shall be given him which will neither enrage him, nor wed you to a man of unequal birth? Think over some plan, and tell me by to-morrow at this time."

So saying, King Burislaf, with the look of a man sorely puzzled, left the Queen and Princesses to themselves, and went off to see some hedging and ditching which his thralls had done for him during the morning.

But he had scarce gone a hundred yards, when he and those of his body-guard whom he had called to go with him on his round, saw a band of men on horseback riding full up to the Grange, which he had just left.

"These men have come far," said the King. "Their horses are jaded, and they themselves travel-worn. Let us turn to meet them; may be they bring a message to me."

"They be Danes," said the King's chief huntsman. "I know them by the golden boar which their leader wears on his steel cap."

When the horsemen met the footmen King Burislaf bade them welcome, and asked the news.

"Our welcome would be a welcome indeed, King Burislaf," said the warrior who led the band, "were we free to take it. We have ridden far, and need rest and food; but King Sweyn, my master, bade us not tarry a moment after we had reached your dwelling, but to tell you his message, and to turn back."

"We are not so courtly, nor perhaps so great a king as King Sweyn, but never has this happened to us that any man who bore a message, least of all if it be one from a king, should turn away from our court without tasting food or drink. The bees of the Wends make sweeter honey than you can find in your Danish beech-woods, and we have better mead, though not such strong ale as King Sweyn brews at Sleswig."

"My master, King Sweyn," said the Dane, "forbade us to stay one moment. So soon as we had given you our message we were to turn bridle and ride back."

"Before you give it, what may be your name?" asked the King. "We cannot take a message from a nameless man."

"At home, in Denmark," said the Dane,

"they call me Sigurd the Champion, and for my office, I am head of the King's Guests."

"And what may a 'guest' be?" said Burislaf. "It seems to be a different thing in Denmark from our guests, for you are a guest, who will be no guest."

"The king's guests," said Sigurd, "are fed and paid servants of the king; freemen whom he takes into his service as messengers. He sends them hither and thither to do his service, to bear a message, or do an errand, cut off a foe, or help a friend. At any time and any whither we are bound to go at the king's bidding."

"And Sigurd the Champion," said King Burislaf, "what is this message of King Sweyn's that will bear such little delay?"

"My master, King Sweyn," said Sigurd, "bids you pay him the tribute which King Harold Bluetooth laid on the Wends in the time of your father Myeczyslaf before the last night of Yule is out, what we, now that we are all Christians in Denmark, call Twelfth Night, and should you fail to pay it he will waste your kingdom with fire and sword."

As he uttered these words Sigurd and his companions turned bridle and rode off, and, jaded though their horses were, they were soon out of sight.

"Mount and follow and slay them," cried King Burislaf. "Was such a message ever heard? And as for the tribute, though years and years ago there was talk of such a thing when our father and King Harold were at war, it has never been paid, and, by God's help, never shall."

As for pursuing and slaying the bearer of that rude message, Burislaf's chief huntsman and the rest of his followers convinced the King that his case would not be mended even if he seized and slew Sigurd and his companions. In this respect the person of a messenger, like that of the heralds in later days, was looked on as sacred.

"Your majesty may kill the messenger," said the chief huntsman, "but you cannot kill the message. Let them go as they come. They can bear nothing back to King Sweyn, for they would not stay to learn whether you would pay the tribute."

"So Burislaf let them fare back on their long journey to King Sweyn, and, instead of looking after his thralls' work, went back to the Princesses' bower, and told them of this new trouble that had come on him."

"Misfortunes never come singly, father," said Astrida; "and this message of the rude King Sweyn only makes it more needful to devise some scheme which shall at once put off both Sigvald and the King. By to-morrow at this time we will all meet here, and each of us bring the best counsel we can."

CHAPTER VII.

ASTRIDA'S GOOD COUNSEL.

How Burislaf or his Queen or the other Princesses passed the night no chronicler has told. No doubt the King caroused with his men, and then snored out the night-watches, as was the wont of Kings when at peace in those days. Perhaps he asked his oldest councillors about that mythical tribute, what it was to have been . rings of gold, Anglo-Saxon silver pennies, Cufic money; so many hawks, so many sables, so many horses, so many swords. If so, the answer of his chancellor of the exchequer has not been recorded. We may be sure that even if he arrived at a clear understanding as to what the tribute should be, he went to bed even more determined not to pay it than ever. If the worst came to the worst, it was a far cry to Stargard. King Sweyn might come and take the tribute if he chose. By this time the Wendish mead had its way, and King Burislaf was sound asleep. In his dreams he fancied, so far from paying Sweyn a tribute, that he, at the head of the Wendish host, had invaded Denmark, slain King Sweyn with his own hand, and offered him up as a spread eagle to Bielbog and the ancient gods.

By his side lay his once proud and haughty Queen, fretting at the thought that any king should thus insult the husband of a princess of the race of Ruric.

" At Novgorod," she thought, " foreign princes and savage chiefs paid tribute to us, and now Burislaf is told he must pay tribute to King Sweyn, who but a little while ago was his own father's exile and outlaw, and would have been glad to find an asylum on our shores."

How Astrida passed the night the following pages will show. She had, as we have seen, both the pride of her mother and the wit of her father. She was not the woman to pass the night in vain hopes or in idle lamentation.

When the royal family met in the bower next day, Astrida was fresh and lively as a bird, while

Burislaf and the Queen were sullen and care-worn.

"Well, father," said the Princess, "have you thought of a scheme first for Sigvald's answer, and next for King Sweyn's tribute?"

"I have thought of King Sweyn," said the King, "and the end of my thought is that I will not pay the tribute. Why, the oldest of my followers cannot tell me even what it was to be. Can a king pay a tribute when its very kind is unknown to him? No! If Sweyn wants the tribute he must come and take it."

"That I call no counsel," said Astrida. "If that tribute is not paid or met in some way, as soon as the paths are open and the waters loosed next spring, you may expect King Sweyn here, sword in hand."

"I know of no other plan," said King Burislaf, gloomily. "In old times my ancestors would have offered up a hundred or two victims at the altars of the gods, and so would most of my subjects at the present day; but we are unbelievers, you know, half Christian half heathen. We cannot sacrifice to the ancient gods, and we are not Christian enough to believe what Otho's mass priests tell us of the power of incense and prayer."

"The best offering to any of the gods, heathen or Christian," said Astrida, "comes out of one's own head and heart. Good counsel comes to man in all creeds if he will but trust in himself, and not in idols and vain oblations."

"Very true, no doubt," said Burislaf, with a puzzled look. "But tell me first what counsel you have to give about Sigvald the Viking, for that concerns you most nearly. If he takes any of my daughters he will take you, for it is easy to see that he will take the best."

"I have thought it all over," said Astrida, "and, as the saw says, it is good to slay two birds with one stone, I have devised a plan which may get rid of Sigvald, or, if we cannot get rid of him, at least relieve us of the tribute."

"If you can do that, either or both of them, you will do something that quite passes my wit to comprehend; but let us hear what it all comes to."

"Well, then," said Astrida, "when Sigvald comes you must make him and his men merry and welcome, and not spare either ale or mead. Your tables must groan with food, and your hall be filled with every man you can muster. There is still some valour left in the Wends, and your body-guard may well compete, at least in looks, with Sigvald and his Vikings. As for ourselves, we may not be so brave as Sigvald, but we shall see if we cannot match him in wit. I say outright that I have no wish to wed at once. Even a princess has many chances, and as yet I have not had one. It is quite uncertain whether Sigvald's choice will fall on me; but whichever it falls on of us sisters, this must be your answer, and you must utter it like a king of our ancient race, and as though you had the whole nation at your back. You must say that the daughters of King Burislaf are worthy of husbands, better born and of higher rank than the captain of a band of Vikings, even though he be an earl's son. But for all that, as you love and value him, and know how brave and how wise he is—mind you do not leave that out, father—you will not utterly say no. Only, if he wishes to have one of us, he must not ween he can have us for the mere asking, just as if we were apples that the wind shakes off the tree to fall into his mouth. No! The daughters of King Burislaf must be won by adventure and enterprise, and you will lay on him a task and quest which may seem great to others who are not so wise and daring, but which will no doubt be easy to such champions as Sigvald and his Vikings."

"And what task shall I lay on him, daughter?" said Burislaf.

"Have patience and you shall hear," said Astrida. "You know the way of the Northmen, when they have anything to say they do not say it outright. Sigvald will linger over his wooing like a cat over a mouse, and all the more so as he will take time to look at us three. Do not be in a hurry with him, therefore. Give him time, and say nothing of his wooing till he mentions it himself; but when he does speak, mind and say all that I have said. And now for the conditions, which, if he is at all taken with any of us, he will be the readier to accept, for love, they say, makes all things easy in a lover's eyes."

"Yes, yes!" said Burislaf. "The conditions:

I am as impatient to hear them as any lover himself could be."

"The first condition of the match must be," said Astrida, "that he shall set the land free from all taxes and tributes which the Wends may be called on to pay to any foreign king. If you put it in that way he will think it a light thing for him and his Vikings to meet such a claim; but do not tell him that King Sweyn has claimed the tribute. That is the first condition, and I am sure he will jump at it, if he is as wife-willing as he is said to be. The second is harder, and how it is to be done even I fail to see; but it all depends on the love that may spring up in his heart for any of us at first sight."

"And what is that?" said Burislaf.

"This," said Astrida. "You shall speak of it as not at all hard. Far from it; you must talk of it as if it were quite a thing of course to such famous warriors and bold sailors as the Vikings of Jomsburg, to whom it is well known nothing is impossible. Sigvald must bind himself to bring King Sweyn hither to us before the first night of Yule, and to bring him so that he shall be in our power. If he will undertake to do that, then he shall have his choice out of any of your daughters ; and do you know, father," said Astrida, " though I am not so husband-eager as Sigvald is said to be, if he can only bring King Sweyn hither I shall be quite ready to wed him myself."

" What a jewel of a daughter," said Burislaf. " My own child, only far more deep-witted. Not Bielbog himself, nor Swantevit adored in Rugen, who knows all counsel, could have devised a better plan. We shall get rid of Sigvald, that I see ; but how we are to get rid of Sweyn and the tribute, that I do not see quite so plainly."

" We shall get rid of both, father ; or if we only get rid of the King and his tax, and keep Sigvald, we shall have done great things. And now go and prepare the feast, and look to your men's dress and arms. Spare no pains or cost ; and even if the last butt of mead be broached, never mind, if we only keep the Vikings in good humour, and play Sigvald off against the King."

So King Burislaf went off that day to look after his thralls' work, and he was in such good humour that none of them smarted for idleness ;

and after that he and his followers rode round the country summoning his men to the feast; and, in a word, made everything ready on the grandest scale that his resources afforded for the entertainment of the Vikings.

CHAPTER VIII.

THE VIKINGS AT KING BURISLAF'S COURT.

Now the story goes back to Jomsburg and the Vikings. The day after the muster was spent in preparation and selection. Amongst Sigvald's fifty followers we may be sure all the chiefs went, though one of the greatest, Bui the Stout, was left to take the command while the Captain was away. It was a strange thing and worth mention, as proving how completely all feuds of family were sunk in the allegiance paid to the Captain by every member of the band, that Bui the Stout, the sturdy son of Veseti of Bornholm, had won all that golden spoil which filled those two chests, of which he spoke at the muster, out of a raid which he had made on Strut-Harold's house not long before he joined the band. But as soon as he was admitted into the company, perfect peace ruled between Sigvald and himself. His gold he still guarded as the apple of his eye, and wherever he sailed those chests went with him. By land, on horseback, they were not so easy to move, each weighing more than one ordinary man could lift. Bui, therefore, was ready enough to stay behind, but, as we have said, most of the other leaders went to Burislaf's court, and among them Vagn and Beorn the Welshman. It was a feature in the movements of the Northmen in that age that any form of travel suited them. If the waters were open they could sail, and so we find them in England and France pushing their long ships far up the Seine, the Thames, the Exe, and even the Stour to Canterbury. On land, when they left their ships, if there were horses to be found, they rode, and in all the Northern hosts the only man we hear of who did not ride was Rollo, the founder of the Duchy of Normandy, and he only did not ride because he was so tall, and his legs were so long that the garrons and cobs and ponies of that age were not high enough to carry him.

Thus it was that those indefatigable hosts flew like lightning from one part of England or France to the other ; and it was this equestrian spirit which we find afterwards developed into the trained chivalry of the Normans. But when there were no horses to be had every Northman could march. They stood on their own legs, as they said, and these never failed them.

The Vikings of Jomsburg, fifty-one of them, under Sigvald, could have found their way to Burislaf's Grange, not quite so fast, but just as surely, as Gangrel Speedifoot; but as their neighbours, the Wends, had horses, and, indeed, as many of the band had horses of their own, on the morning of the second day after the muster Sigvald and his men took horse at early dawn, and at dusk had put the forty miles or so which lay between Jomsburg and Stargard behind their heels.

The country through which they rode was varied. Now their way passed over great moors and plains, now through forests of fir and oak and linden and ash, growing more and more wooded as they approached the King's Grange, which presented the appearance of a large farm in a clearing of the forest.

At the gate of the Grange King Burislaf's marshal and his attendant thralls met them, and helped them to dismount. In an out-house stood wooden buckets of water, in which they washed off the traces of travel; and it was remarked that there was a good store of towels on which to dry their hands, a towel for each man, proving that the Queen and the Princesses and their women had not been idle with their spinning wheels for years and years before.

"The Captain," said Beorn, "when he brings back his wife will bring a good portion of linen with her. This is just as it is by the laws of the good King Howel in Wales, who ordained that no maiden should presume to marry till she had spun linen enough for her wedding sheets and enough besides to deck her husband's table."

"She will bring back more than linen," said another. "The Wends have always been famed for their mead and their wisdom. Let us hope she will bring good store of both into Jomsburg."

"You are a better judge of mead than of wisdom," growled Beorn, "and so I trow is the Captain, or he would never have come on this wild goose chase, breaking the law."

"Hold, hold," said the other. "'Tis now you that break the law, since yesterday the law is changed you know, and now any of us may take to himself a wife with the Captain's leave."

"All!" said another; "but you forget, Karl the Red, that before any of us gets that leave he must do something to deserve it."

"Well, then," said Karl the Red, whose face was covered with a thick red beard, "I hope the day will soon come, when this marriage and feasting is over, that we may go out for an autumn cruise, and then see if I do not distinguish myself, for, to tell the truth, I am quite as set upon marriage as the Captain."

"The Captain is not married yet," said Beorn. "What says the saw, 'Many a slip 'twixt the cup and the lip,' and so it may be in this case."

By this time these ablutions which, we are sorry to say, were performed with very little soap—that being a great luxury—were over, and the King's marshal now came to conduct the guests to Burislaf's hall.

It was a building exactly on the pattern of that of the Vikings. In the middle burnt the fires, along the sides ran the double row of benches. As you entered the hall from the door, quite at the end of one side, the King sat in state, on the right hand in the middle, in gay coloured garments, with his coronet of gold round his head; right and left on either hand were his councillors and warriors, among whom Gangrel Speedifoot was conspicuous, in the precedence of their rank. But there was this difference between the King's and the Viking's hall, that while the high seat or raised chair over against the King was reserved for Sigvald and his fifty followers, the Queen and the Princesses, and their ladies and waiting women, sat up on a raised bench at the end of the hall opposite to the entrance, in a position which exactly answered to the high table on the daïs in the mediæval halls.

Behind the King stood pages in bright holiday clothes, with wax-tapers in their hands, a piece of luxury which the Wends owed to their wealth in bees. In the North, tallow, or more commonly still, long resinous strips of pine-wood, served instead of wax. Pages also stood behind the Queen and the Princesses, who might be described as sitting in what passed in those times for "a blaze of light." All down the length of the hall stood thralls with torches in their hands, and altogether, if between the fires and the torches there was much smoke, it could not be denied that there was more fire in the hall, and that King Burislaf's banquet seemed every thing that was warm and bright and comfortable to the Vikings, who had ridden all the way from Jomsburg, who were both famished and thirsty, and in whose hall at home wax was unknown, torches seldom used, and where the horns of mead went round to the low dull light of the fires which warmed the building.

Up the hall strode the marshal, followed by the Vikings, who wore their best attire, which consisted chiefly in wearing blue or red, instead of the more sober russet of their daily garb. Every man carried his sword by his side, for it was an unheard of thing to enter even a friendly hall entirely unarmed. Their broad axes and spears and bows and quivers and shields were left behind in the out-house where they had first entered, and now they stood a goodly band of fifty most tall and proper men at Sigvald's back before King Burislaf in his high seat.

Fine feathers, they say, make fine birds, and King Burislaf, in his high seat, in his royal robes, with his coronet on his brow, looked a very different man from him who had turned two days before to hear King Sweyn's insulting message. He was short of stature, as we have said, but he had that good fortune, which so becomes a king who has to sit in state, that his body was long in proportion to his legs, and so when he sate in his high seat, he looked taller and more majestic than he really was.

As Sigvald came before him, the Viking Captain bowed his head gracefully but proudly, and said never a word till the King spoke first and said :

"Welcome to our hall, gallant Captain. Welcome, both you and your brave Vikings, who are the mainstay of our state and the defence of our coast. Take the seats of honour opposite in the order of your rank, and eat and drink and enjoy yourselves as much as you can under our royal roof."

"Thanks, noble King," said Sigvald. "We heartily accept your bounty and your good cheer," and with these words, after another low bow, the Captain and his followers took their seats on the benches opposite.

As soon as the guests were seated, a host of thralls brought in tressels and boards, on which the food was served; when they had been arranged and decked and covered with linen, in which again the luxury and the industry of the Wendish Court shone out, another crowd of thralls bore in the joints, roast and boiled, of beeves and boars and deers, which formed the feast. After these had been despatched, the bones, we are sorry to add, for the sake of the manners of those days, being picked clean with the fingers, and then thrown beneath the table —a custom which, be it remarked, was continued in civilized Italy until Dante's time—the thralls again bore in what were called kickshaws, cakes, and puddings, in which women delighted, but which the full-fed warriors passed away from them by a sign. Eating over, and before the serious drinking of the evening began, the guests had time to look about them, and to scan, through the glare of the torches and the smoke of the fires, the faces and features of the Queen and Princesses at the upper end of the hall. It was not then the fashion for ladies to eat in public. For them those were the days of luncheon or snacks, which they took at odd hours in an uncomfortable way in the afternoon. Though they were present on state occasions in the hall, they did not partake of anything except the kickshaws, in the making of which the Queen and the Princesses had a great share. After the eating, they were present when the great toasts to the gods, or to the guests, were drank, and after that they speedily and gracefully retired, leaving the men to their ale and mead, and to that wassail and merriment, in song and story, which lasted till far on into the night.

On this occasion, as soon as the boards were cleared, the King's butler, who was no thrall but a freeborn Wend, stalked up the hall, clad in a red kirtle and tight-fitting blue hose, and, standing before King Burislaf, reached out to him a huge horn of mead.

Up rose the King in his seat, and, bowing towards Sigvald over against him, who rose as Burislaf rose, called out :

"I drink to the health of Sigvald, Strut-Harold's son ; to him and the Vikings that bear him company. They are all right welcome on Wendish soil."

Then, half draining the horn, he gave it back to the butler, who bore it across the hall, and handed it to Sigvald, who, in his turn, raised it aloft, and said :

"I drink to the health of the noble King Burislaf, Lord of the Wends. Long may he live, and long may he rule this land. In this toast all my brethren in arms join as one man."

A murmur of applause followed this speech on the Viking side of the hall, and their joy was complete when thrall after thrall flocked in bringing horns of mead, which they handed to the Vikings and the King's men alternately, one horn to each pair of men, who rose and pledged each other from opposite sides of the hall.

When this toast-drinking was over, all eyes were turned to the cross bench on the daïs at the top of the hall, for all the Vikings, and Sigvald the foremost, were anxious to see something of the Princesses, one of whom was the cause of their coming.

But they should have looked before. They were too late. In the midst of that revelry of toasts and pledges, the Queen and her daughters, and their women, had passed out of the hall, and

King Burislaf and his men and their guests were left to finish their carouse alone.

It was one consequence of the King's state, and of the arrangement of the seats, that nothing like conversation was possible between the King and his guests. There the fifty-one on one side sate over against the fifty-one on the other, talking among themselves, and draining their horns of mead, but without a word of common intercourse.

"This is dull work," said Beorn to Vagn. "The food is good and the mead equals our own, but for all the mirth and amusement we get, we are far better off at home in Jomsburg than in King Burislaf's hall."

Whether the King thought it dull himself, or whether what followed was part of his plan, certain it is, that he beckoned to his butler, who in turn whispered to the marshal, who went out of the hall, and soon returning went before Burislaf and said:

"May it please your Majesty, your two bluemen are ready to wrestle on the floor."

"Let them approach," said the King, "and let us make merry over their feats of strength."

Then the marshal spoke to the butler, and the butler to the warder at the gate, and it was thrown open, and two negroes, or "blue-men," as they were called in that age, came bounding into the hall. Their woolly heads were close shaven, and they were clad in tight vests and short hose, that they might wrestle with each other with less hindrance.

It was a barbarous spectacle, but not worse than the prize-fights which still sometimes disgrace this age. The two blacks flew at one another with the fury of wild beasts, butted at each other with their heads, and buffeted one another with their fists, grinning and howling horribly all the while. Then, coming to close quarters, they wrestled with one another for a long time, till one gained the mastery, and, with a dexterity which either Cornwall or Cumberland might have envied, sent his antagonist flying over his head with a fall which left him stretched on the ground without motion. The victor then squatted down like a huge ape on the chest of his fallen foe, who was at last dragged out of the hall, giving little signs of life, by the thralls, who laid hold of his heels, while the conqueror was rewarded by King Burislaf with a horn of mead, which he swilled down with the greediness of a brute, and, throwing a somersault, ran off out of the hall amid the cheers of the Vikings, who were amused and delighted with the exhibition.

"Whence do they come? What are they? Are they men or apes?" These were some of the questions which ran round the Vikings, only to be answered by Beorn, and some of the veterans, that they were a kind of wild men who lived in Africa, where the sun was so hot that it turned all the blood in their veins black, and then their faces grew black as well.

As to how King Burislaf had got possession of them, all the butler could say was, that the Emperor at Bizantium had sent them as a present to Burislaf, when Gangrel Speedifoot came home from the East, and that Gangrel said he would not care to lead two such monsters, valuable and rare as they were in the West, through Russia again. No! not for all King Burislaf's treasures.

After this entertainment, which was very successful of its kind, King Burislaf's minstrels followed, and sang to their harps the glories of the Wendish race, and how their kings in particular had come down straight from Heaven to found their dynasty; but as the music, as Beorn said, was very monotonous, and not to be compared to the songs of the Welsh harpers, and as, besides, the words were in the Wendish tongue, which few or none of the Vikings could understand, that part of the entertainment was not thought nearly so pleasant as the wrestling of the negroes; and, to tell the truth, Sigvald, and some of his band, began to yawn terribly over their cups.

Perhaps Burislaf saw them across the hall, perhaps he guessed it of himself. But however it was, when the minstrels had at last finished their interminable music, he sent them about their business with a horn of mead, and after they were gone rose and said:

"The gallant Captain and his band may well be tired after their travel. To-morrow, too, we must rise early to hunt the boar and bear and wolf. The wax tapers are getting short, the logs smoulder on the fires, if you have well drunk it might be well to retire to rest."

"We have both well drunk and well feasted,"

said Sigvald; and then he added, with a courtesy which well became him, "the wrestling of the blue-men and the strains of the minstrels have delighted both our eyes and ears. Thus sated with food and mead, and with feats of strength and the sweetest melody, we may well say that nothing more is wanting to ensure us a good night's rest."

Then Burislaf rose and strode out of the hall in great state, preceded by the butler, and followed by his followers, while the marshal and thralls waited to lead the Viking chiefs to the various outhouses, where they were to sleep, by twos and threes in a room, a long loft over one of the stables being reserved for the dormitory of the rank and file.

These were not the days of tea and coffee, of headaches and dyspepsia. In a few minutes every man in and about the King's Grange was sound asleep, except the one or two who had to sit up and keep watch and ward over the King and his goods.

Next morning Burislaf and his men were up early, nor were the Vikings missing from the morning meal. Much the same state was observed, the King sat in his high seat, with his men on his side, and Sigvald with his followers on his. The food and drink was much the same, except that any who chose to abstain from ale or mead might drink milk or milk mixed with honey. The Queen and the Princesses did not appear, and until they chose to show themselves, however impatient Sigvald might be, there was no use in asking after them. That would have been regarded as highly improper in that age, quite as much so, in fact, as if King Burislaf had all at once asked his guests what was the business on which he came, though he well knew what it was, or how long he meant to stay! In those days nothing was considered so impertinent as curiosity, and nothing so inhospitable as to let it be supposed that a guest was not welcome to stay in your house for ever if he chose.

When the morning meal was over, King Burislaf and his men led the Vikings into the wide woods which enclosed the royal farm, and there all day, and till it grew dark, they bayed the bear, slew the boar, and chased the wolf, having good sport with all their game. With the bear Vagn especially distinguished himself, for when all the rest had left the forest, he turned back to fetch his cloak which he had thrown off and forgotten. As he sought for it he came upon a huge brown bear, not in the sweetest mood, which made at him. But Vagn was as strong as a bear himself and as cool as any bear as well. He threw his cloak over the bear's snout as he rushed at him, and, turning aside at the same time, got behind him while he was entangled in its folds, and with one stroke of his sword cut off the whole snout just below the ears. Then picking it up he walked off with his cloak, leaving Bruin to reconcile himself to his position as best he could. When he rejoined the company they were just about to turn back to look for him, Beorn, the Welshman, at their head. But when they saw him dawdling along with the bear's snout, or rather half his head, in his hand, King Burislaf and the Wends burst out in wonder at the youth who could cope with a bear single-handed, and even the Vikings and Beorn, slow to praise one of their own company, all declared that there was none among them who at a pinch was better than Vagn, Palnatoki's grandson.

"If the Captain, foster-child," whispered Beorn, "brings down his game as well as you have brought down your bear, he will be a mighty hunter of women; but here we have been a whole day tracking them, and as yet we have scarcely seen the game."

"All in good time," said Vagn, "all in good time. Women are more wary than bears, and don't rush at a young man with a cloak as soon as they see him, like yon snoutless bear. As soon as Sigvald sees them, he will trap them, or one of them, take my word."

But for all that there seemed little chance of their doing more than seeing the Princesses at a distance. When they met at the evening meal, there sat King Burislaf in his high seat, as stiff as his royal robes could make him; there came the marshal to lead Sigvald to his place, and there sat the Queen and her three daughters and their ladies on the cross bench on the daïs.

As the Vikings were not so hungry nor so thirsty as they had been the day before, they had more time to look about them, and the eyes of Sigvald in particular often wandered towards that end of the hall; and as they were both long- and sharp-sighted, he soon made up his mind that the tallest of her daughters, who sat next the Queen, was at first sight the fairest of the three. This was Astrida, of whom the reader already knows something, but of whom, up to that time, Sigvald knew absolutely nothing, except that one of Burislaf's daughters bore that name.

The feast that night went on in much the same way as that of the day before. The boards, when brought in and spread, groaned with food, and there was no stint in drink. After the meal, the King stood up and pledged Sigvald and the Vikings; the Queen and Princesses and their ladies disappeared, and the minstrels began their monotonous strains. But the Bluemen, or Blackamoors, did not appear, for the very good reason that one of them lay with three broken ribs after the struggle of the last night, and his companion had no antagonist with whom to contend.

"'Twill be livelier in Valhalla, if we ever get so far," said Beorn. "If things bide so dull as this, we shall have to quarrel with some of these Wends, just to keep up our spirits."

"What think you of the Princesses?" said Vagn, when that observation was made.

"What I think of all women," answered Beorn; "fair to look on, and foul to take. No man knows what it is to have a real enemy till he has a woman for his foe. All the harm in the world comes from them."

"But the world could not exist without them. Had you never a mother, Beorn?"

"Yes," said the Welshman, "but she was as good as dead before I was born, for I never knew her."

"Or a wife?" asked Vagn.

"Yes; but she ran off with an Englishman, while I was away on a Viking voyage to Ireland, and wasted my goods—all, that is to say, that she did not take with her. That was quite enough for me. I never took another."

"But some might be good," rejoined the young man.

"Aye, that's just it," said the old woman-hater. "They might, but they are not."

"Which of these Princesses now do you think the Captain will choose?"

"My eyes are old, and I can see better to bend a bow and steer a ship than to pick out the fairest of three women; but to my mind the tallest—she that sat next to her mother on her right hand—had the best of it in looks."

"She looked proud as Freyja herself," said Vagn; "but for all that she is not so fair as Ingibeorg, Thorkell's daughter. Do you think she will take the Captain?"

"Take the Captain?" retorted Beorn, "of course she will. Setting aside his brother Thorkell, Sigvald is the tallest and fairest of the band, quite as comely as you, foster-child, and withal an older and a more proper man. If we talk of taking, it would be rather, will Sigvald take her?"

"Why he came hither to choose one of the Princesses; what can he do better than take the fairest?"

"Aye, aye!" said Beorn; "but marrying a princess is not so straightforward a thing; Burislaf has no sons, and these three princesses are his heirs. If Sigvald marries one of them, he becomes entitled to a third of this realm on Burislaf's death."

"Then we Vikings of Jomsburg, who have everything in common, will share in this third part of Wendland?"

"True, boy," said Beorn; "and pretty work we should make of it, sharing the land among us, and tilling the soil like thralls, and leaving the burg, and being cut off by the Wends and Germans one by one. That sharing of land would be even worse than bringing women into the burg."

"This question of the marriage must be settled to-morrow," said Vagn; "for I know Sigvald told Bui we should be back on the fourth night. We shall hear naught to-night; see, the King rises to leave the hall, and bids Sigvald sleep sound, as we all shall, after our long day's hunting."

So the Vikings left King Burislaf's hall, and sought their beds, and their first day among the Wends came sleepily to an end.

CHAPTER IX.

SIGVALD'S WOOING AND KING BURISLAF'S ANSWER

NEXT morning at breakfast, when King Burislaf and Sigvald met, the King asked what the Vikings would like to do—whether they would spend it in hunting, or in fishing in the river, or in manly sports.

"We had sport enough yesterday in your royal woods," said Sigvald. "To-day let us think of business, and of my errand hither."

"Eat and drink your morning meal first," said Burislaf. "No business sits well on an empty stomach."

So Sigvald and his Vikings and the King and his men took their seats in the hall, and despatched their meal in silence, for Sigvald was thinking of his wooing, and Burislaf of the clever answer which he had ready for his guest.

When the boards were cleared, Burislaf said to Sigvald:

"Let us retire to my small room, and then I shall be ready to know what business brought you hither."

He said this after he had risen from his high seat; and as Sigvald had also risen, the King and his guest met in mid hall.

"Not so, King Burislaf," said Sigvald. "Not so; my errand, hither, though but partly known to thee, is well known to all my men. The Vikings have changed that head of our law which forbids any of us to take a wife, and my errand hither is to ask the hand of one of your daughters."

The wily King—though, as we have said, he had been informed already of Sigvald's intention—affected great surprise at this proposal.

"A king's daughter, sprung from the royal house of Ruric, and the monarch of the Wends, married to a Viking captain! That, Sigvald, is an offer over which we must think twice. Eagles do not match with hawks, nor ravens with daws."

"An earl's son of Danish race is a hawk compared with the royal race of Ragnar at home, but he is an eagle when matched with a

Wend, however princely," said Sigvald proudly. "As for daws, the ravens of the North are no daws, and I throw the term back in your teeth."

There was a murmur of applause from the Vikings behind him which showed that they were pleased with Sigvald's bold words, while the faces of some of Burislaf's followers turned pale with fear. Even the King himself thought he had gone too far, and that it was time to draw in his horns.

"Be not angry, noble Sigvald," he said. "I only meant to show that this offer had taken me by surprise, and that I had thought to wed my daughters to men of higher birth, high though yours is, and brave and valiant as you are!"

"I came hither to consult you on business," said Sigvald, "and now you know my errand. I await your answer, King Burislaf. To-morrow, after the morning meal, my men and I will mount and ride home."

"Be it so," said Burislaf. "Stay with us to-day. To-night, after supper, you shall have speech and nearer sight of my daughters, so

that you may make your choice. To
morning, before you leave us, we w
you our answer to your offer."

Sigvald could do naught else than accept the King's terms. He and the Vikings spent the day in feats of strength, in which their might and dexterity were the wonder of the surrounding Wends. All that day they saw nothing of the Queen or the Princesses, but in the hall after supper King Burislaf led Sigvald up to the cross bench at the top of the hall, where the ladies, contrary to their practice on the two previous nights, remained sitting.

As they stepped on the daïs, Burislaf turned to the Queen, and said:

"This is the noble Sigvald, who is our friend, and the great safeguard of our coast. He has now told us of his errand hither. His secret is out. He wishes to ask for the hand of one of our daughters."

Though the Princesses heard this, they did not, as perhaps might be the case with modern Princesses, start up and hurry from the presence of that daring suitor. On the contrary, there they sat motionless, two on the right and one on the lists of their mother, who merely answered:

"This is a new and strange thing that an earl's son, and a vassal of our own, should ask for the hand of one of our royal race."

"No vassal, lady," said Sigvald, proudly, "though an earl's son. We Vikings hold Jomsburg, not as vassals of the Wendish King, but by our own good swords. If King Burislaf weens that either the castle or our arms belong to him, let him come and try to take them."

"If not a vassal, though I weened you were one, still an earl's son," said the Queen.

"Earls in Denmark are kings elsewhere," was Sigvald's proud reply. "But earl's son or churl's son, here I am, Sigvald Harold's son, Captain of Jomsburg; and I demand the hand of that Princess who sits at your right. May I also ask whether her name is Astrida, Gunnhilda, or Geira; but whatever name she bears, her I choose, who sits now next to you on your right."

"Her name is Astrida," said the King, "our eldest daughter. Your choice has darted down on her soon, like a hawk among a flock of finches."

"My eyes have not been idle since I sat in your hall," said Sigvald. "Three nights now have I sat in the same hall with Astrida, and all last night my eyes wandered towards her seat. My thoughts had already settled on her before I spoke of my errand this morning."

As Sigvald said this, he would have turned and spoken to the Princess, but this was a step utterly unknown to the court etiquette of the Wends. After Sigvald's declaration as to his deliberate choice, the Queen rose, and her daughters and ladies with her. As they left the hall, King Burislaf said :

"You have spoken your mind, noble Sigvald; and, as I have promised, you shall have your answer in this hall to-morrow at the morning meal. We will do all we can to further your suit, for we look on you and your comrades as the mainstay of our kingdom ; and though the Queen uttered the word, it is not as vassals we look on the Vikings of Jomsburg. But I warn you if we grant your suit it may be coupled with some conditions."

Sigvald's answer showed that even that short glance at Astrida had enchained his heart.

"The Princess is fair as Gerda to look on. Any condition which does not bind me to give up my good sword, like Freyr, will be looked on as light by me."

What Beorn the Welshman, the sworn woman-hater, would have said had he heard this gallant speech, is not hard to imagine, but as Sigvald and Burislaf stood alone on the daïs, after the departure of the Queen and the Princesses, no one heard it but the King, who said:

"Well spoken, noble Captain; spoken like a man and a Viking, ready to win his lady-love by his good sword, and that alone. Be sure, if we lay any behest on you before you get this match on which your heart is set, it will be such as will not require you to part with the sword which has been such a terror to our enemies and your own."

The two then left the daïs, and returned to their high seats, and the revelry and minstrelsy filled out the evening as before.

While the King took counsel of his Counsellors on either side, Sigvald and his brother

Thorkell spoke long about the match. The end of this conversation was that Thorkell said:

"Why, brother, you are so taken with this royal maiden, that you are, after all, like Freyr, and will do anything to get her."

"Everything, brother," said Sigvald, "that may befit my own honour, and the interests of the band."

"May your honour and our interests ever go together, brother; but what a thing this love is that pulls down a man's strong will, as though it were a straw, and fills his soul with fancies, when before, he had thought alone of war and spoil."

"Marked you, foster-child," said Beorn to Vagn, "how flushed and red the Captain's face was when he came back from the daïs?"

"I marked it well," said Vagn, "and put it all down to the good ale and mead."

"Ah!" said Beorn, "that was none of the honest blushes which strong drink brings even into my bronzed cheeks. No! no! but was a blush of shame, caused by the poison called love. Who can tell whether these Wendish women have not bewitched our Captain with their runes and filtres. They are as bad in that way as those Finns we burnt in their wigwams last year, in Helgeland. When love once gets hold of a man, no one can tell whither it will lead him."

Again the feast came to an end, the three nights having been attended with a consumption of drink and food which drove Burislaf's butler and marshal to their wits' end. One of the matters of business on which they talked with their royal master was the approaching end of the stores, laid up in the cellars of the grange, and they were, therefore, greatly comforted to hear that the terrible Vikings were not likely to spend another day with them, but that they would mount and ride as soon as they had drunk their stirrup-cup after the next morning's meal.

"Such men to drink I never saw," said the butler, "and may it please your Majesty, the worst of them all is the oldest of the band. Horns of mead and ale go down his throat like water, or far faster than running water. They call him 'Beorn the Welshman,' that is, in their barbarous tongue, Bear the Welshman, and surely he is a bear at drinking."

"We grudge them nothing; they are our friends," said the King; "but be sure if either meat or drink fail while they are here, you both, our butler and our marshal, will come to grief. I will cut a red stripe out of each of your backs."

"They shall last," cried the butler; "but, please your Majesty, if they offer to stay another day, do not suffer it, for we have not enough left, either of mead or meat, for such another night."

"They will go," said the King in a grand way, "but Burislaf the Wend can never turn any guest out of his house."

So the King arose, and the Vikings went to their rest, and the butler and the marshal passed the night with great dread, lest the unwelcome guests should prolong their stay; but they need not have been in such fear, for Sigvald was eager to get his answer and to depart, that he might fulfil the conditions laid on him, and return and bring back Astrida to Jomsburg as his bride.

Whether he slept sound or not that night is not recorded, but if lovers in those days were like lovers now, it is certain that the Captain of the Vikings could not have had a wink of sleep.

He was up with the lark, looked at his own arms, mustered his men, and made them look to theirs, had their horses brought to the grange from the fields in which they had been tethered and fed on Burislaf's hay and corn. In a word, like a prudent leader, he saw that all was ready for a start after breakfast, and then he sat down with Burislaf in his hall, feeling that he had done a good morning's work, and yet it was not nine o'clock.

What King Burislaf had been about in the meantime does not appear. Perhaps taking stock with his butler of the fearful inroads which the sharp-set teeth of the fifty-one Vikings had made in his cellar and larders. Perhaps in renewed deliberations with the Queen and Astrida. In whatever way he had spent the morning there he was in his high seat in the hall, bidding his guests welcome to breakfast, and ready to speed in every way the parting guest.

There was one new feature in that morning's

repast. It was shared by the Queen and the Princesses, who actually had tables laid before them, and lifted horns of mead to their dainty lips. It was the first time that the Vikings had seen the royal ladies by the light of day, and though very little of that light found its way into the hall through the side slits just below the roof, they had a better chance of seeing them, and taking the measure of their charms, than was possible through the smoke and glare at night.

"Lovely maidens all three," said Vagn, "and the Captain has chosen well if Astrida be that tall one with the raven locks and bright blue eyes; but for all that Ingibeorg —"

Here his ravings about the fair Norwegian were brought to an end by his foster-father, who gave him a thump on the back, as he passed the horn to him, and bawled out:

"Stop! stop! boy, I am sick of Astridas and Ingibeorgs; love-making is no trade for Vikings. I heard the Captain say, if this match were made it could only be on some conditions. I only trust we may be sent on a quest as long as that on which Thor went to Utgard, and that we may be all cut off in it, and go straight to Valhalla, where you know there will be no women, and so never have to bring women and wives into Jomsburg."

At last the meal was over. In the court-yard were heard the champing and snorting and neighing and tramping of the fifty-one horses, which the King's thralls held outside, ready for the Vikings to mount and ride.

It is a dreadful and a dirty thing to think of in these times of universal baths and shirt-changing; but not one of the Vikings had any baggage with him. The clothes they stood in were their best, and they had not brought a change with them. Nor certainly was there a sponge or a tooth-brush among the band. Even towels, one to each man, had been looked on as a great luxury. Verily most dusty, dirty and uncomfortable times.

But to return. The meal was over, when Sigvald rose and said:

"The hour has come, King Burislaf, when we must mount and ride. What answer do you give me to my offer for the Princess Astrida's hand?"

"The answer is ready," said the King.

"May I hear it in private," asked the Captain.

"Not so," said the King with dignity. "Your offer, Sigvald, was made in open hall, in the hearing of your men and mine, and my answer shall be as open, so that all the men may hear it."

"Utter it at once," said Sigvald, "and let me go with my men."

"This is my answer," said King Burislaf; "you shall have Astrida, though, as you well know, I look on it as an unequal match. Whatever you earls may be in Denmark, we in Wendland think earls far below kings. But as you are a tall, proper man, the captain of a great company of valiant warriors, and so powerful in men and money as to find few your match in the North, we are willing to give you my daughter's hand on two conditions. The first, that you set Wendland free from any tax or tribute that other kings may claim from us; the second, that before the first night of this next coming Yule, you bring King Sweyn of Denmark with you to this grange, and place him in our power, to do what we like with him. If you cannot do both these things, then, Sigvald, you shall not have my daughter's hand."

That was what King Burislaf said, and it was plain, from the crest-fallen faces of Sigvald and his Vikings, that they felt themselves very much in the position of the Norse gods in Asgard, when one of them was asked to put his hand into the Wolf's mouth; or like Balder, when the mistletoe flew through him. For a moment or two neither Sigvald nor any of his men said a word. Then, after he had recovered his speech, he said:

"Set Wendland free from any tax or tribute that any King claims! Who claims any tax or tribute from thee, O King?"

"That we do not tell you," said Burislaf, "you must find that out for yourself, and when you have found it, make the King that claims it give it up."

"And then the second," said Sigvald; "how am I to bring King Sweyn hither?"

"That I am sure I cannot tell," said the crafty Burislaf. "All that I say is, that you have asked for Astrida's hand, and those are the conditions. You Vikings cannot be the great and brave men you are said to be, or to be so deep-witted as some of you claim to be, if you cannot do both these things."

"Does the Princess agree to this?" asked Sigvald.

"Listen to her own words," said Burislaf. "Astrida, you have heard what I have said. Do you agree before all this company to become Sigvald's wife, if he sets our country free from any tax or tribute which other Kings may claim from us, and if he brings King Sweyn of Denmark hither, before the first night of the next coming Yule, and place him in our power?"

"I do," said Astrida.

"Then," said Sigvald, "I accept the terms. Before next Yule, King Sweyn shall be here, and after that I will set this land free from tax or tribute, so help me all the gods, and if I do not, then I forego my claim to Astrida's hand."

By this time the Vikings had recovered their self-possession, and a roar of applause followed the bold words of their Captain, in which even the Wends joined.

"Nothing then remains, noble Sigvald," said King Burislaf, "than that you should drink your stirrup-cups and mount and ride. Astrida, bear a horn of mead to the noble Sigvald, and bid him good speed on his journey and his quest."

"With all my heart," said Astrida, as she handed the horn to her suitor.

After he had drained it, Sigvald turned to her and said,—

"Long before the first night of Yule, King Sweyn shall be here, or I will die in the attempt to bring him, and when that is done, the tribute will be an easy thing."

"No doubt," said Astrida, "and if you will take counsel from me, you will be sure to bring him first. You may find then that it will be far easier to rid us of the tribute."

Then Burislaf thanked Sigvald for the honour he had done him in coming so far to see him, and Sigvald thanked him in return for his royal bounty and hospitality, and the Vikings took horse and rode home, rather puzzled to know whether their journey had been successful or not.

CHAPTER X.

THE CAPTAIN TAKES COUNSEL.

THE very next morning after his return Sigvald called together his chiefs, and especially Bui the Stout, the stern Viking, who would not leave his chests of gold, and so had stayed behind to rule the garrison.

When he laid the matter before them they all agreed that if anything was to be done in the matter it must be done quickly. Though September was passing away, they might be sure that the news of the conditions laid down by King Burislaf would sooner or later reach the ears of King Sweyn, and when that happened their enterprise would be tenfold more difficult. Nor, strong though they were in men and ships, were they at all a match for the united strength of Denmark, if any cause, such as an attack upon the King, combined the nation in self-defence.

If King Sweyn were to be caught and

trapped it must be by guile and cunning rather than by brute force, but by what stratagem no man could tell.

All this time Beorn the Welshman chuckled, as might be supposed, and declared that Burislaf had completely worsted Sigvald in the trial of wit, and had laid on him conditions which no man could fulfil. "Bring Sweyn to the King's grange!" he constantly repeated; "it is all very well to say bring him, but how is he to be brought;" and, indeed, that was the opinion of Bui and all the band. It would be easy to provoke King Sweyn to battle, and, perhaps, to conquer his fleet and take him prisoner; but then, perhaps, he might defeat them, and then the company would be ruined, merely that Sigvald might marry a princess. The end was that nothing came of their deliberations, and Sigvald was left very much to his own resources, and became for a day or two rather a laughing-stock to his men. He got wan and pale, and wandered about in deep thought, and Beorn, whenever he saw him, held up his hands and said to Vagu, his constant companion,

"See how true it is all that I said of those Wendish philtres and runes. Take my word for it, Astrida has bewitched him."

So two days or more went on and Sigvald was as far off his end as ever, when one day Gangrel Speedifoot walked into the burg almos unchallenged, as the warders knew him wel and once in he came straight to Sigvald lodging.

"I have a message for thee, O Captain he said, "and it comes from the Prince Astrida, who says she has thought over yo matter, and this is how you must act if you w bring King Sweyn. She is sure this is the wa it must be done, for she dreamt it in a dream- and she is a clear dreamer—and this is what sl dreamt: "It seemed as though you had set sail your ships for Denmark to fetch King Swey and that when you got to Zealand you f ill and were so sick that you could not lan and that you sent for King Sweyn to co on board ship to you, and lo! he came—a suddenly, before he could set his foot on sho again, a great wind arose and carried the sh and you and him in it to Jomsburg, and when you had him in Jomsburg it was an easy matter to bring him to King Burislaf. She bade me also tell you, that it is King Sweyn and none else who claims tax and tribute from King Burislaf, so that if you should be able to catch him in that way, you may kill two birds with one stone, and fulfil both the conditions at once. In token of all this she has sent you this golden ring, which you saw on her finger as she handed you the horn that morning."

That was Gangrel Speedifoot's message, and it is easy to see how very happy it must have made the Captain. Why had Astrida taken all this trouble, and told him the best way to fulfil the conditions and win her hand if he had not found favour in her eyes by his bold suit for her hand ?

"Say nothing to any of the band about this," said Sigvald to Gangrel Speedifoot. "Fill your pockets with these gold pieces and find your way back to the Princess as soon as you can. Stay ! bear this ring too as a token from me, and say that within one month—and that seems a very long time—I will either bring King

Sweyn to King Burislaf or perish in the attempt."

So Sigvald and the messenger parted, and no one knew of the Princess's message but the Captain.

Next day Sigvald summoned his chiefs again to counsel, and said—

"I have now thought over this matter of King Sweyn, and how to catch him with little risk, but I cannot tell you the way in which I mean to seize him, except that if it fail, and I perish in the attempt, it will be with little loss of life. I will only take three ships with me, and one hundred men in each. They need not be our largest ships, as they will have to lie close up to shore."

"We do not ask," said Bui, "what your plan is. We trust you thoroughly, and have no doubt that if your wit cannot devise some plan to catch the King no one else can. Only remember, that if you perish all the band will have a blood-feud against King Sweyn, for we are all brothers in arms, and each bound to avenge the other."

"Thanks, Bui the Stout, and spoken like the

noble warrior you are. Believe me, I have every hope that you will neither have to waste your gold chests in paying a ransom for me, nor will the band lose strength by any deaths among my crew. I mean to win the day by cunning only, and to bring King Sweyn hither without losing one dop of blood! But as things turn out variously, and it may be fated that I should die on this voyage, I leave the captainship of the band to thee, Bui, while I am away; and as for thee, Beorn, and thee, Vagn, I pray you both to come with me to share in this hunting of a king."

"With all my heart," said Beorn; "it is nigh two months since I sniffed salt-water and saw a foe. My arms are all rusty for want of use while we waste our lives idly at home. It will do Vagn good too to see his own land, even though he is now an outlaw of King Sweyn."

So it was settled that three ships and three hundred men should go, and that Sigvald, Beorn, and Vagn should steer each a ship with a crew of one hundred men.

As the war-snakes ran out of the harbour,

the walls and arch over the entrance were crowded with Vikings, who longed at once to be with them, and wished them a speedy voyage and a safe return.

The weather was mild and fine and the sea smooth, as it often is at that time of the year in the Baltic. Sigvald and his little squadron sped swiftly over the waves, as the rowers plied their oars, and it was not long ere they neared the Sound and ran into the Belt between Fünen and Zealand, on which latter island they heard that the King of Denmark was at one of his granges.

It fortunately happened, that though King Sweyn was at enmity with some of the Vikings, and more particularly with the house of Palnatoki, he had no quarrel with Sigvald or his father, Strut-Harold, who was one of his great earls, and so looked on the Viking captain rather in the light of a friend than an enemy. Even, therefore, if he heard that Sigvald had been seen in the Danish waters the news would not have alarmed him, and he would expect a friendly rather than a hostile visit from the Viking captain.

All this Sigvald had reckoned on, and made it part of his bold scheme. As soon as he knew precisely where the King was he ran his three ships boldly into an inlet where there were none of the King's galleys, and then made his men practise the old plan of Palnatoki, by which they lay with their sterns towards the land and their prows out to sea, so as to be ready to dash forward as soon as the oars touched the water.

This done, now came the most difficult part of the adventure, which Sigvald had adopted pretty much after the advice of Astrida. He knew the King was feasting in his hall hard by with six hundred men, and that as soon as he heard of his arrival he would expect to see him. But with his three hundred men against the King's six hundred he could not expect to do much. If his purpose were carried out at all it must not be carried out by force.

There sat the King in his hall, which was arranged very much like that of the Vikings and King Burislaf, only on a grander scale, drinking with his men, until the warder spoke to the marshal and the marshal to the butler, and the butler stood before the King and said :

"A message, O King! from Sigvald, son of Strut-Harold, Earl of Scania."

"His messengers are welcome," said the King. "Let them approach."

Then Thorkell the Tall, who also went with his brother, strode up the hall, the wonder of all the Danes for his huge stature, and came and bowed before the King.

"Welcome, Thorkell," said King Sweyn. "Speak quickly; which will you do first, drain a horn or tell your errand?"

"I will do both," said Thorkell; "for both can be done quickly."

Then he seized the horn and drained it, and had scarcely swallowed it before he said:

"My brother Sigvald craves speech of your Majesty, for he has matters of great moment to tell you."

"Craves speech!" said King Sweyn with an oath. "Why then does he not come and speak himself? Why send you as his messenger, tall though you be?"

"Because he cannot leave his ship," said Thorkell. "Yonder in the bay he lies bedridden on board. We ran out of Jomsburg three nights ago to seek you, and on the way Sigvald has fallen sick, and is now so weak that he is at the point of death; but before he dies he desires to see you, and so he has sent me to bear the tidings."

"Know you what he wishes to say?" asked the King.

"Know! not I," said Thorkell. "Sigvald is a man who ever keeps his own counsel, and shares it not with others."

"But is he so bad?" said the King. "Must I go down to the bay this very night to hear his words?"

"The morning sun will scarce see him alive," said Thorkell. "He seemed at the last gasp when I left. I trow it was something about Jomsburg and the captainship that he wished to speak about."

"I daresay—I daresay," said Sweyn, now thoroughly bent on going. "Something that concerns us much. We will go."

So the King, followed by two hundred men, and the twenty which Thorkell had brought with him, left the hall and the amber mead and went down to the creek in the bay where Sigvald's ships lay.

When they reached the shore, it was only to find a change in the arrangement of the ships. They now lay lashed together end on, so that the two that lay nearest to the shore were as it were a jetty or bridge to reach the third, in which the sick Sigvald lay.

As soon as Sigvald heard that they were approaching the shore, he took to his bed and heaped the clothes over him.

"In which ship is he?" asked the King.

"In the third," said Thorkell; "and as our ships are small and light, do not take more than thirty men with you on board them, lest they should sink under us."

"So it shall be," said the King; and up the gangway he went into the first ship.

As soon as ever thirty men had stepped on board her Thorkell made them pull in the gangway and cut the ship off from the land; and when the King with twenty men had gone on board the second ship, the gangway in that was also pulled on board, and that also cut off from the first. So with the third, when the King and ten of his men had set foot on board of her, in was drawn the gangway, and the third ship was cut off from the other two, which at the same time slipped their moorings, while the rowers sat on the benches ready to start.

When the King—who suspected nothing, for it was dark, and he was well drunk—got on board the third ship he asked where Sigvald was, and was told he was in the cabin at death's door.

"Has he his speech?" asked the King.

"He has, Lord," was the answer; "but he is very weak."

"Make haste!" said Sweyn, "that I may hear what he has to say before he dies."

The ships in those days were half-decked, or rather decked at stem and stern. The stern rose high up into a poop; under that deck the Captain slept.

The King went into the cabin where Sigvald lay in his berth, and leant over him, and said:

"Can you hear my voice, Sigvald? Tell me what you have to say."

But Sigvald said never a word.

Then the King spoke again.

"What are these great tidings which you

have brought me hither to hear, for I am ready to listen to them? Speak, Sigvald, speak."

Then a low thin voice came out from the pile of clothes under which Sigvald lay, and the King could just make out—

"Bend over me a little, Lord, and then you will be better able to hear my voice, for it is now very low."

Then the King bent over him, and as he did so Sigvald threw one arm round his neck and took him with the other round his waist, and held him with a grasp of iron, which showed how little weak he was.

So he held him fast, and at the same time called out as loud as he could to his crew to fall to their oars as fast as they could, and row out of the bay. And so they did on board all three ships, and carried off the king and his thirty men captive, and left the rest of his followers standing staring on the shore.

CHAPTER XI.

KING SWEYN IN JOMSBURG.

All this time Sigvald held King Sweyn fast, and even if he could not have held him, there close by stood Thorkell the Tall ready to give help; but, in truth, Sweyn, Viking though he had been, and strong though he was, was no match for Sigvald, and so the captain held him easily.

As soon as Sweyn recovered his first surprise he said:

"What! Sigvald! will you play me false? What mean you by this treachery? Great tidings are these in truth; but, after all, I do not see why you should treat me thus, who have been ever friends with your father, Strut-Harold."

"No treachery is meant, Lord," said Sigvald; "but it will be good for you, as well as for us, that you take a little voyage with us to Jomsburg."

"To Jomsburg!" said the King. "I never meant to fare so far when I got out of bed this morning."

"Very true, Lord," said Sigvald; "but no man, not even a king, can tell when he rises at morn where he shall lay his head at even. Your father thought to trap and kill you at dawn, but before the sun rose Palnatoki's arrow rattled through him from midriff to mouth, and he fell dead, and you rose to the throne."

"Chance and Fate rule all things, it is true," said Sweyn; "but why I should fare to Jomsburg I cannot see. Will you throw me into a dungeon and put another on the throne?"

"Not so—not so," said Sigvald. "Be sure, Lord, we will pay you all honour, and treat you in every way as becomes a king. Our hall in Jomsburg is not so grand as yours at Hedeby or Viborg, but so far as our poor means go, you shall lack nothing. You and your men shall be welcome as old Vikings and brothers in arms."

"With some of you old Vikings I have lost no love of late years," said the King sullenly. "Beorn, the Welshman, Palnatoki's foster-brother, will exult when he sees Sweyn, the son of Harold Bluetooth, brought in as your captive."

"Captive, Lord, is not the word," said Sigvald. "Not captive, but King of Denmark, though in Jomsburg."

"King of Denmark, indeed," said Sweyn, proudly; "but why a King of Denmark should be thus carried off by guile to Jomsburg passes my understanding."

"You will understand it well enough, and how all things will turn to your good and glory when we reach Jomsburg," said Sigvald. And as he said this he let go his hold of the King and set him free; and he and King Sweyn went out of the cabin on to the poop. By this time the three war-snakes had made a good offing in the smooth sea. As the King turned to the shore there he saw the lights burning through the windows of his hall, and he thought of the strange ups and downs of fate, which in so short a time had snatched him away from his kingdom and his men, and given him over into the hands of those who might either turn out to be his friends or his enemies.

Sigvald seemed to read his thoughts, though he could scarcely see his face.

"Yes, Lord!" he said, "there burn the lights as we can see; and there too, though we cannot see them, tramp your men back to the hall, to tell how the mighty King Sweyn, the son of Harold Bluetooth, has been carried off by the Vikings of Jomsburg."

"It is a daring feat," said Sweyn, "and so long as the North is inhabited by men shall this story, how Sigvald carried off Sweyn, be told in your praise. I am ready to confess that I have been worsted in this trial of wit; by arms I could have held my own, but against guile no shield is proof."

"Let us think and talk no more about it, Lord," said Sigvald. "Of this be sure that not a hair of your head shall be harmed, and if you will only see things when you are in Jomsburg in the light that we see them, you shall return to Denmark very shortly a greater king than you left it."

"I trust I may," said Sweyn; "but how that is to be is another thing that passes my understanding."

"All will soon be made clear, Lord!" said Sigvald, "and now let us drain a horn of mead, and after that, may it please your majesty to retire to rest in my poor bed, the best I have to offer you."

King Sweyn, as we know, had not always been a king; and if he had been, kings in those days were not for ever lapped in luxury; it was no privation, therefore, for him to sleep on the narrow bed in which Sigvald had so lately lain to seize him. Added to this, he was young and hopeful, and though all was dark before him, he saw at once that the best thing to be done was to believe all that Sigvald said, and to treat the Vikings as his friends so long as they were friends to him.

For the rest of the voyage, therefore, he was merry and gracious. As the rowers, five and twenty on a side of the long-ship, gave their backs with a will to the work, he was full of praise at their dexterity and sturdiness. Whether like Olaf, the son of Tryggvi, then an exile before Earl Hacon, but afterwards, King of Norway, he showed his agility by running along the blades of the rowers' oars when their stroke was in full swing, is not recorded ; probably not, and yet King Sweyn was foremost in his day for such feats of strength and skill. All that we know is, that Sigvald carried him off, as we have said, and that on the morning of the third day the three long-ships ran into the harbour of Jomsburg, and thus Sigvald had as good as performed the first of the two conditions which were to make Astrida his wife.

Great was the excitement of the Vikings on the burg when the warder blew his horn, and summoned the Captain to the arch over the entrance, whence he scanned the open sea.

"There be our ships yonder," said Bui the Stout, "safe enough ; but have they sped on their errand, and is King Sweyn on board them, or has Sigvald perished, and come these ships back to tell us?"

"'Tis too soon yet to say whether the flag at the mast-head is red or black," said the warder. "The Captain told me before he sailed, that if he had seized the king he would fly a red flag, and if he failed the ensign would be black."

Then a little further on he called out, "I see

the flag now as it flies out from the truck, and it is—yes, it is red as blood. Shout, boys, in triumph," he cried to the Vikings, who now thronged the arch, "for the Captain has well sped, and in that foremost ship he brings King Sweyn with him as his captive."

At this we may be sure the Vikings shouted, and, then in a little while they ran down to the mouth of the harbour, to throw wide the iron gates, and to hail the Captain and his comrades as they shot into the port.

As Sigvald ran alongside the wharf, Bui the Stout stood ready to greet him.

"Welcome home, Sigvald, son of Strut-Harold," he said. "There is no need to ask how your reward has sped, for I see it in your face. But where is the King? Have you brought him alive or dead?"

"Alive, and not dead, Bui the Stout," said Sigvald, "and not a drop of blood shed either of his men or ours."

"All power to your head as well as to your arm, Sigvald," said Bui. "Sure, none of us is a match for you in wit."

"Say not so," said Sigvald. "In this, too, as

in most things, chance rules, and not the wit of men."

"But where is the King?"

"In my cabin," said Sigvald, "and ill at ease, though he wears a cheerful face."

"No wonder—no wonder," said Bui; "not for all my gold in both my chests would I stand as he now stands."

"He said," Sigvald went on, "he would not stand on the deck to be a sight for our men when we ran into the port, and so he sits in my cabin. But mind, I have given my word that no harm shall happen, either to him or his men, if he will only do what is best both for him and us."

"We should be dastards and truce-breakers if we behaved ill to them in any way," said Bui, "and so I am sure all the band will feel, though, to be sure, it is a great feather in our caps to have caught the mighty Sweyn, King of Denmark, and carried him off to our castle of Jomsburg."

"Come on board and see him," said Sigvald. "Your father, Veseti, and he have long been friends, and, remember now the old friendship how Sweyn stood by you in your quarrel with my father, Strut-Harold, when you spoiled our goods."

"Will that scar never be filled up, I wonder," said Bui. "I thought it had been long since forgotten."

"So it has, so it has, Bui the Stout," said Sigvald. "I only thought of it to your good. Have not the laws of this great company done away all blood-feuds between us? Are we not bound to avenge one another as though we were born brothers, as well as brothers in arms?"

"True, true," said Bui, "and yet that old quarrel passed through my mind, and also this, that you are about to break the laws in one point. If we break them in one, they may be broken in all."

"We break them in one point because times change, and it is good now to marry, though it once was not. But the law that binds every one of us to avenge another of the band as his born brother, must abide for ever. So long as the band lasts, that law must abide."

"So long as the band lasts, that is the point," said Bui.

"Point, or no point," said Sigvald impatiently, "come on board and greet the King, and let us lead him to our hall."

Then Sigvald and Bui went into the cabin, and led King Sweyn out of the ship to the common hall, while the Vikings gathered round to gaze at the great king, who had, at one time, been a Viking like themselves, and the boldest of sea-rovers; nay, had even been the brother in arms of Beorn, the Welshman, and the foster-child of their old captain, Palnatoki.

Nor was Sweyn unworthy to be matched with any man in that stalwart host. Singularly well made, broad across the shoulders, slender in the waist, of that lithesome make which so often conceals far greater strength than at first sight appears; he was, in stature, every inch a king. If Burislaf were rather short and squat, Sweyn was far above the middle height, and, except in a band where every man's stature was dwarfed by such giants as Thorkell, King Sweyn would have been called tall. Besides this, his hair was light brown, flowing in curls down his back, his eyes were large and of a deep blue, his features were straight, and his mouth open and winning. At heart he was sullen, crafty, and revengeful, but he had no opportunity of displaying the first and last of these qualities in Jomsburg. On the contrary, he was open, and genial, and confiding, and soon won the hearts of the Vikings, who, as we have said, looked on him as almost one of themselves, and a glory to the craft. Even Beorn, the Welshman, who owed him such a grudge for his enmity to Palnatoki, was taken by the King's condescension. Sweyn had not seen him on the voyage, as, though the three ships steered on the voyage in company, no man passed from ship to ship; but as they walked in a sort of procession up to the hall, the King picked out the veteran from the captains, who bowed before him to do him honour, and called out—

"Well met in Jomsburg, old messmate; where was it we last parted?"

"In your hall, Lord," said Beorn, "after the arrow went round, and I went back into your hall to look for my man."

"True," said the King, "but that was in anger. We had parted in peace before."

"Whether it were peace, or whether it were

war, I scarce can tell," said Beorn. "All I know is, that it was on the morning after Harold Bluetooth fell, and we Vikings said that we had all helped to let the rat out of the trap."

"Both that and the arrow shall be forgotten," said Sweyn. "Let bygones be bygones, Beorn, the Welshman. Our blood-feud ceased when Palnatoki died."

"Spoken like a king," said Beorn, "and whatever come of it I will ever be on your side."

"Spoken like an old messmate, Beorn," said Sweyn; "but where is Vagn, Palnatoki's grandson? I would see if the bear's cub takes after the old Bruin."

"He is not far off, Lord, for he is here," said Vagn, who stood at Beorn's elbow.

"King Sweyn looked at Vagn for a moment, and said:

"So this is Vagn, who, when only sixteen fought with Sigvald and made him yield, and so won his way into this gallant company. Denmark is proud of you, Vagn, son of Aki. Do you never long to return to Fünen, and settle down on your own estates?"

"I am over young to settle down, Lord," said Vagn. "A Viking has no home; like the bird in the air or the fish in the sea, his home is wherever spoil and fame are to be found. Like the bird or the fish, he follows his food wherever it may be found."

"But the day may come," said Sweyn, winningly. "I, too, have been a Viking. You may wish to wed, and I know no Viking is allowed to take unto him a wife."

"There," said Beorn, "you are, for once wrong, Lord, for the law has just been changed in Jomsburg, and any man may now marry with the Captain's leave."

"When was the law changed?" said Sweyn, in amazement.

"Scarce ten nights back," said Beorn.

"Then," said the King, "I look for Vagn back to Denmark sooner than I had thought. He will marry, mark my words, and when he marries he will come back to Fünen."

After these words the King passed on to the hall, and Sigvald led him to his own high seat, where he had his morning meal, for it was still early in the day. There we leave the King to himself till the time comes for the great feast, which the Vikings have to make for Sweyn in their hall that night.

CHAPTER XII.

THE FEAST IN THE VIKINGS' HALL.

NEVER had so grand a feast been held in Jomsburg, but though short the time to prepare it, those were not the days of French cooks and made dishes, and the magnificence of a banquet consisted rather in the number of the joints and game of various kinds, and in the abundance of the drink, than in anything else.

But for all that it was a grand and solemn banquet, and in one thing it surpassed all others ever held in the burg, it was graced by the presence of a mighty king.

There in Sigvald's high seat sat King Sweyn, in the robes which he wore when he had been snatched away. By his side sat, right and left, the chief of the men who had been captured with him, who had not yet recovered their astonishment at the success of Sigvald's stratagem. Over against the king sat

Sigvald in the high seat opposite, and on either side of him were on the right Bui, and on the left Thorkell the Tall. All the chiefs of the Vikings and their best men, to the number of two hundred, were in the hall in their best and brightest clothing, collars of gold and silver ornaments, strings of beads and gems, the spoil of many voyages, hung round their necks; and their arms, inlaid with gold on hilt and haft, bespoke the success which had ever attended that famous company in fight.

It so happened that the only weapon which King Sweyn had with him when he was seized was a light battle-axe, meant more for show than work. This Sigvald had soon discovered, and before the feast began, he stepped across the hall and said:

"Though it is unlucky to give a friend steel, I trample the ill-luck under my feet, and give thee this sword, Lord, which I took away in Ireland in the west, out of the cairn of an old Viking."

As he said this, he held out the sword and belt.

The King looked at it, and saw it was a thing

price; a treasure which even a king might ar. The hilt and pommel were rich with ld and precious stones, and it had a silver abbard, tipped with gold. The peace-bands or rings which held it in its sheath were of olden twist.

As the King held out his hand and grasped the hilt, he said:

"There is no ill-luck, Sigvald, Harold's son, in giving or taking a sheathed sword. It is naked steel that cuts love, unless the giver first draws his own blood before he gives it. But a sword bound by peace-bands, as this is, a king might take and a captain give, and yet their friendship would be never the worse."

All this the King said in a loud voice, so that all in the hall might hear.

"Gird me now with the sword, Sigvald," said the King.

Then Sigvald girded him with the sword, and the King called out again, so that every man heard:

"Now hath Sigvald, Harold's son, girded me with his own sword, and done homage, in token that I am lord over all this band."

There was a roar of voices at this among the company; but Beorn said to Vagn, "By this trial of wit the King has got the best of it, for he has treated Sigvald as though he were his marshal or steward, and had girded him with his sword in sign of homage."

If the same thought struck Sigvald, he said nothing about it, but slowly returned to his high seat, and taking a horn from his butler, drank to the health of King Sweyn, Harold's son, who had honoured the Vikings by paying them a visit to Jomsburg, and accepting a banquet in their hall. Having half drained the horn, he passed it over to the King, who finished it, and in return gave the health of Sigvald and all the band.

After that the feast went on in the usual way. There was hard eating and deep drinking, even while they were at meat; but at last even their appetites were satisfied, the tables were cleared away, and the horns and mead remained behind. There sat the King with the torch-bearers behind him, the observed of all beholders, and over against him sat Sigvald and his captains.

There was a pause, and Sigvald seemed rather at a loss what to say, but in a minute or two he came to himself, and rose, and said in a voice just as loud as that in which the King had spoken :—

"Right glad am I, and right glad are we Jomsvikings, Lord, to see you here at our head ; and though that sword with which I girded you a while ago, was not meant as an act of homage, still I am willing, and we are all willing, that it should in part be taken as such. We Vikings of Jomsburg owe allegiance to no man. So long as we are in this burg, we belong to it, and it belongs to us. Out in the world it is otherwise ; and when I am at home in Scania, or Bui in Bornholm, or Vagn in Fünen, or Beorn in Wales, we each of us owe allegiance to the King of those lands, and are in so far his vassals. In one way, therefore, we are vassals, we chiefs each of us of King Sweyn, and in another not. But for this time at least, now that King Sweyn has been so good as to visit us, we will not quarrel about words, but will own that for this once we are all his vassals."

There was a murmur of applause, answering to the modern "hear! hear!" at those words of the Captain, and every one listened what he would add to such a clever beginning.

"It may seem to you, Lord, both that the manner of your coming hither was strange, and that what I have done was done without a reason. But it was not so. You talked of homage, and I talked of vassals; but what is worse for the vassals of any land—though I must say, I thought all Danes were freeborn men, and no vassals—what is worse for vassals or freemen than to see that their king will not take to himself a wife, and that should anything happen to him, as happened, we all know, to Harold Bluetooth, he would die and leave no heir to the throne. And now I come to the reason which led me to Denmark, to seek the King and to bring him hither. King Sweyn, Harold's son, hath been too long unwedded, and my eyes have spied out a princess who is worthy of his hand: in fact, she is by far the best royal match in all the North. Let the King say the word and take her to wife, and he may be married, as his people desire, and we all desire, and be back at his hall in Zealand long before the first winter night."

Here the wily Sigvald paused, to let his Butler fill his horn. Then he raised it high in air, and half draining it, passed it over to the King, calling out as he did so :

"This horn I drain in honour of the Queen of Denmark!"

As King Sweyn took the horn, which it would have been the greatest slight to his host to refuse, he said, with a very puzzled look :

"I may well drink this toast to the Queen of Denmark, my queen that is to be one day or other. This binds me to nothing, to drink to a nameless queen, and sooner than spare your drink, Sigvald, Harold's son, I drain this horn, declaring that I never yet heard of a king who was given away to a woman whom he had not yet known."

As he said this, King Sweyn drained the horn, amidst the shouts of the Vikings ; and then Sigvald went on :

"I am well pleased that King Sweyn has fulfilled the wishes of his subjects and vassals, and all his freeborn folk at home and abroad, and has plighted his troth to the princess of whom I spoke. If he wishes to know her name, he shall have it at once. It is Gunnhilda, and she is daughter of Burislaf, King of the Wends, with whom and his forefathers the Kings of Denmark, as we all know, have had some dealings. Fill the horns," he roared out, "to the health of Gunnhilda, Queen of Denmark! but as the King has not yet heard her name, he shall not drink the toast, though, unless he learns to like her, I am afraid he will have to stay longer than I expect in Jomsburg."

These last words were not lost on King Sweyn. He knew that he was in a trap now, just as much as when Sigvald held him in his iron grasp, and that he could not leave Jomsburg except at the Captain's good pleasure. He rose therefore as soon as Sigvald had ended, and said:

"Bring hither the horn, and let it mantle high; I will drink to the health of Gunnhilda, Queen of Denmark!"

If the Vikings had shouted with joy before, they were ten times as noisy now that King Sweyn had yielded to their Captain's will. The

King raised his horn in air, and up went all the horns at the same time, and "Gunnhilda! Gunnhilda! Queen of Denmark!" rang through the hall.

"He has swallowed the hook, brother," said Thorkell, "which you so skilfully baited. He is now in your hands. You may do with him what you will."

When the uproar had abated, King Sweyn rose, and said:

"Though I cannot compete with Sigvald in his glib tongue, I may still crave leave to say a few words. As is well known to all of you, this match is none of my seeking; nor would I have chosen a Wendish princess had I been left to my own free will. There has never been any love lost between the Danes and Wends; and, besides, I have just claimed from King Burislaf the tribute which my father Harold laid on his father Myeczyslaf, but which has never been paid. Still, as Sigvald has been so good as to choose for me, and as you all know I am here in a cleft stick, what can I say but that I will take the maiden if she be fair of face and hale of frame."

Having said this, King Sweyn sat down amidst the applause of his hosts.

Then Sigvald rose again, and said :

" I would never have set my eyes on a princess for you, King Sweyn, had she not been both fair and strong. There are some here who think Astrida, the eldest daughter of King Burislaf, the fairest of the three, but for all that Gunnhilda, the second, is a princess in every way fitted for the throne. It is not right, therefore, to look on this match, which we have chosen with much care, as though it were one of force or need. True it is, O King, that you have come against your will to Jomsburg, but that was only to bring you to the princess, and in no sense are you here as a captive, but as a king."

"Say no more," said King Sweyn. " This is not the bed on which I should have chosen to lie, but here I am in it, and I must be content with it, be it long or short, easy or hard. I have given my royal word to wed Gunnhilda, if she is fair and hale. I am ready to go to King Burislaf's Court to-morrow, that I may be the sooner married, and the sooner get back to my kingdom."

"There, again," said Sigvald, "I am constrained to speak a word against the King. No doubt he is burning to fly to see this fair lady; but princesses, fair as she, are not to be frightened. I must first go before the King to herald his coming, and when that has been done we will lose no time in bringing King Sweyn to the Court of King Burislaf."

By this time the King was weary of the marriage and of the debate, in which it seemed that Sigvald was to have it all his own way.

"Bring me a horn of mead," he said, "and let me wash this marriage out of my throat, down which it has been forced. I will give you a toast, Vikings, in which you will all join, I am sure: 'May all your marriages be as lucky as mine, now that you have broken your old laws, and are all eager to marry.'"

Round went the Butler and the thralls, up went the horns, and down went the foaming ale and mead. "May all our marriages be as happy as King Sweyn's," was the cry, and then there were no more speeches and no more wrangling, but drinking long and deep, till, as the Saga says, King Sweyn and Sigvald the Captain, and all the Chiefs of the Vikings, and every one in that hall went well drunk to bed.

CHAPTER XIII.

HOW SIGVALD WENT TO KING BURISLAF.

Now we leave King Sweyn, a king in name, but a captive in condition, within the walls of Jomsburg, treated with honour, but watched as jealously as an infant, while Sigvald rode off in triumph to King Burislaf to say how well his errand had sped.

King Burislaf, as we know, was in no great hurry to see Sigvald again. He wished, if he could, to be rid of both Sweyn and the Viking Captain, though, as is clear, he could only get rid of one at the expense of the other. It was with no very pleasant feelings, therefore, that he saw the company of Vikings, with Sigvald at their head, again riding up to his Grange; and his Butler and Marshal groaned, when they thought of the fresh inroads which the new-comers would make on their stores.

But there was no help for it. There they

were, and the Wends had to make the best of them.

"How many days, Gangrel Speedifoot," said the King, "is it since they were last here?"

"Barely fourteen nights," said the swift runner. "Sigvald, Harold's son, equals Thialfi in the fleetness of his feet."

By this time the Vikings were in the court of the Grange. Thralls hurried forward to hold their stirrups and tend their horses, and King Burislaf greeted Sigvald as though he were overjoyed to see him.

"What news, what news from Jomsburg, noble Sigvald? Is all well with your band?"

"All is well," said Sigvald; "but as for tidings, more has happened since we parted than a fasting and a standing man can tell."

"True! true!" said the King. "Here, you thralls, lead the noble Sigvald to his lodgings, and, as soon as he has bathed his limbs, lead him to our hall."

While Sigvald retired Burislaf went into the Queen's bower, and, holding up both his hands, exclaimed,—

"Here has that furious Viking come back again, and he has so much to tell that he must wait to eat before he utters it."

"Back again so soon!" said Astrida. "Has he brought King Sweyn with him?"

"King Sweyn with him?" said both the King and Queen in amazement. "Why should you think that he could do such a thing?"

"Because a while ago I dreamt a dream," said Astrida; "and methought Sigvald came hither, and brought King Sweyn with him."

"Dreams always go by contraries," said the King. "Why that was the very feat which we laid on this Viking, because we thought it would be too hard for him."

"Sigvald is a proper man," said Astrida, "and a crafty and a bold withal. To such a man all things are possible."

"Well!" said the King, "women, as is well said, are as a turning wheel. One cannot tell what they will say or do. Not a fortnight ago you thought Sigvald beneath you, and were all for putting him off by laying a quest on him which he could never carry out, and now you say he is a proper man, which no doubt he is, and bold too; but, as for craft and guile, that we have got to see."

"I feel, for all that you say, as though I should be the Captain's wife, for you must keep your word if Sigvald fulfils the conditions."

"Of course, of course," said King Burislaf; "but what is the use of talking about it, when, no doubt, he has come to tell us in a long story that he gives up the match."

"That, something tells me," said Astrida, "he will never do."

"We shall soon know," said Burislaf; "and now put on your best attire all of you to grace the banquet. Thank the Gods, there are but ten of them come this time to eat us out of house and home."

"Something tells me, too," said Astrida, "that you will have to make a feast soon that will waste all your stores of meal and mead and flesh."

"Something is always telling you 'something,'" said Burislaf. "Such another feast as we made fourteen nights ago for these sharp-toothed Vikings, and we shall never be able to make both ends meet through the winter."

But, though close and stingy in his heart, nothing could have been more hospitable and generous than King Burislaf in his hall that evening. Wax-tapers blazed, mead flowed, boards groaned, and minstrels sang.

When the boards were cleared, the King rose as before, and drank to the health of Sigvald, who had again honoured him with a visit.

"Such a friend," he said, "he was always glad to see. The more so, as he was sure that he would not have taken the trouble to ride so far had he not some news which it concerned the Wends to know."

Sigvald rose, and drank to the King in return, and then said,—

"Not much has happened in Jomsburg since we parted, but much out of it."

"Not much in, and yet much out," repeated the King. "You speak in riddles. Speak out, man, if you have aught to say."

"I will," said Sigvald haughtily. "No news has happened in Jomsburg, but in Denmark King Sweyn is missing."

"King Sweyn missing! Since when and how have the Gods taken him to themselves."

"The Gods have not taken him," said Sigvald. "He has been missing from Denmark since I took him five nights since, and carried him off to Jomsburg, where he awaits your majesty's pleasure."

"King Sweyn in Jomsburg," cried out Burislaf; "and awaits my pleasure. Strike up, minstrels, your loudest and most joyful strains, for now the ancient foeman of the Wends is delivered into my hands."

"How say you, King Burislaf," shouted Sigvald across the hall, "have I fulfilled one of the conditions which you laid on me that I might win your daughter's hand."

"All but," said the King; "the bargain was that you should bring him here into our power. He is not within it, so long as he is shielded by the Vikings of Joms."

After this piece of news the feast went on for a while, till the King rose, and said,—

"What you have spoken, noble Sigvald, is right and fit to be uttered in open hall, but there are things behind which we will wish to know more privately; rise, therefore, and mount the daïs, and sit beside the Queen and the Princesses, and tell us how you seized King Sweyn."

This was much after Sigvald's mind, and a few steps brought him and Burislaf to the daïs, preceded by the taper-bearers. As he stood before the ladies, his eyes grew bright and his face flushed at the sight of Astrida, and it was easy to see that her charms had not been without their workings on his heart.

As he bowed before the Queen, he said, speaking to her, but in reality at Astrida,—

"Gracious lady, one of my conditions has been fulfilled, more by the clever counsel of others than of myself. King Sweyn is now in Jomsburg, honourably treated, as is seemly, by the band, and he only awaits your pleasure."

"'Twas a bold deed, and not wrought without bloodshed, no doubt?" said the Queen.

"So far from that," said Sigvald, "not a drop of blood was shed in the adventure. King Sweyn was taken by cunning, and by a stratagem revealed to me in a dream."

"Sit down, sit down," said Burislaf. "It is ill standing after a feast, and makes the head swim and the eyes weak. Sit down, and tell us how you trapped King Sweyn."

So Sigvald sat down between Astrida and the Queen on the cross bench, and the King and the two other Princesses with them, and he told them the whole story, which, as they already know it, we will spare our readers.

When the tale had come to an end, King Burislaf said,—

"And when will King Sweyn come hither that we may have him in our power?"

"That," said Sigvald, "depends altogether on your majesty. If you will do as I advise, King Sweyn shall both come hither, and you and the Wends will be set free from that claim of tribute, for it is to him that you are asked to pay it, and besides, gain great honour."

"Say on," said Burislaf; "we are ready to hear, though at this hour of the night our head is wont to nod. Do you therefore, Astrida, who are the wisest of us, mark well what Sigvald says, and be sure you remember it all to-morrow morning."

"I shall be sure to remember it, father," said Astrida, whose blue eyes smiled on the manly

Sigvald, and showed that they were now both on the same path and understood each other.

"King Sweyn shall come hither;" said Sigvald, "but I will not bring him to be mocked and made a prisoner, to be maimed and thrown into a dungeon, as has been the fashion of your Wendish Kings. If he comes he shall come as a King to a splendid feast, guarded by three hundred Vikings, and every inch a King. He is my liege Lord in Denmark, though I am his host and captor in Jomsburg, and I will not bring him hither on any other terms."

"That is a proud bidding," said King Burislaf, who had already begun to nod. "Proceed, I pray."

"King Sweyn shall come to a feast, indeed," said Sigvald, "for it shall be his wedding feast. He is as eager to marry as I am, and he has fixed his choice on Gunnhilda, the second daughter of the King."

Here Gunnhilda started as much as Princesses in any age are allowed to start, and the Queen looked frightened. As for Burislaf, he only snored, for the strong mead had mastered him, while Astrida smiled as she thought what a clever, crafty man Sigvald was.

"But suppose," she said—for in her father's absence of mind she was spokeswoman—"suppose we accept that as a fulfilling of the first condition, and that we suffer King Sweyn to wed my sister, what becomes of the second condition, how are we to be set free from this claim of tribute that King Sweyn has made?"

"Very easily," said Sigvald; "I have thought of that, too, and this is what I think; King Sweyn, when he marries Gunnhilda, must make her a morning gift the day after they are wedded, and his morning gift shall be this claim of tribute on the Wends, which his father Harold Bluetooth laid on, but which has never yet been paid. He will give up something which is nothing worth to him, but worth everything to you Wends to be rid of."

"What a jewel of a man you are," said Astrida; "now I see it all as clear as day. I see that I shall be Lady of Jomsburg, a prouder title than that of Queen, while you, Gunnhilda, will be Queen of Denmark, a throne on which any Princess of the North might be proud to sit."

"Yes," said Gunnhilda; "it would be a very proud thing, if it did not come on me quite so suddenly. Here am I, never thinking of marriage, and I am to be made a Queen, whether I will or no."

This was a very long speech for the second Princess to make; and as she uttered it she looked imploringly towards her mother. Those stern, haughty lips parted for a moment only to utter in accents that chilled all love,—

"No one asked me whether I liked it when I was given away to King Burislaf."

Then Astrida went on,—

"And when do you think King Sweyn will come? I am so anxious to see my royal brother-in-law."

"I have already told you," said Sigvald, "that King Sweyn awaits your pleasure. He is eager to come himself, for all the band have told him of Gunnhilda's charms, eager to be married, and not least of all, eager to get home again. It had best be soon, or else the Danes may come hither to look for him, and then, perhaps, there might be some talk of a real tribute."

"I see it all as you see it, Sigvald," said Astrida, which we mark as the first time that she called him "Sigvald," and he marked it as well, and blushed just as much as a Viking and a man of honour was allowed to blush in those days, which was not often, and very little at a time.

"The sooner," she went on, "this match takes place the better. There will be no peace for any one while this matter of King Sweyn is unsettled."

"After the morning meal to-morrow," said Sigvald, "I mount and ride for Jomsburg; on the second night from that expect me with King Sweyn to his marriage feast."

"I said only to-day to my father," said Astrida, "I was sure there would soon be a feast which would consume all our winter stores, but I own I was not thinking of a royal marriage. But what our Butler and Marshal will now do, I am sure no one can tell. They will be at their wits' end, and we may have to move to another Grange, as this is almost eaten out.

But let them see to that, we Princesses and our women must look after our wedding clothes. Fortunately, my mother has pell, and bawdekyn and sammit, and cloth of gold enough to fit us both out like the daughters of a long line of kings."

Here King Burislaf started up, and we are sorry to say gave the back of his head a great knock against the wooden bench.

"What is all this," he cried, "which I seemed to hear between the humming of the mead in my head? Pell, and bawdekyn and sammit, and a royal marriage, and King Sweyn coming hither? Astrida, mind you be ready to tell me all about it; and now, Sigvald, let us go to bed. Beshrew me, if I recollect anything of what has happened this evening, except what you told us in the open hall, how you had caught King Sweyn, and had him fast in Jomsburg, awaiting our good pleasure."

And then, after the Queen and Princesses had retired amid the salutations of Sigvald, King Burislaf staggered off to bed, and Sigvald sought his chamber, where, if he had any time for reflection before sleep seized him, he must have been overjoyed at the success which had hitherto attended his enterprise to win Astrida's hand.

CHAPTER XIV.

HOW SIGVALD RETURNED TO JOMSBURG.

NEXT morning King Burislaf was up betimes. After his first heavy slumber he had a weight on his mind which could only be relieved by Astrida. He knew that he had missed some news of importance, and was impatient to hear it.

Luckily, Astrida was as impatient to tell what had passed as he to hear. At early dawn, therefore, the father and daughter had met, and Astrida had told her story in the way most likely to further her own plans, which were now to become Sigvald's wife.

As she went to the conference with her father, she caught herself saying,—

"Why, he is as tall and fair and strong as the Northmen's Sigurd Fafnirsbane, and as wise as Heimdall; what more could a woman wish? And as for King Sweyn, Sigvald has vanquished him once in wit, and will vanquish him again."

"What was all that about a royal marriage," said Burislaf, when they met, "and pell and rich stuffs and feasts? I really thought we had feasts enough lately."

"I told you only yesterday I felt sure we should soon have a much grander feast, and so it will be when King Sweyn weds Gunnhilda."

"Sweyn marry Gunnhilda!" cried Burislaf. "Well! well! I do just remember that Sigvald said something about it; and what did I say?"

"Say?" said Astrida; "why, what all must say, that you thought it a very good match and quite to your mind."

'Did I say as much as that? What a thief mead is of a man's wits! I don't remember a word of it!"

"Quite as much," said Astrida.

"And what did your mother and Gunnhilda say?"

"Gunnhilda said it was a match made rather in haste, and my mother rebuked her by saying it was always the way with royal marriages, and that no one asked her if she liked it when she married you, father."

"That is very true," said Burislaf. "It was all done in a hurry, for we had war in the land with Harold Bluetooth, Sweyn's father, and we could not wait; but a match is like a pancake, the sooner it is made and swallowed the better. And now, Astrida, tell me what did you say?"

"Oh!—I said—I said—I said I thought it would be a good match for all of us if King Sweyn gave up the claim to the tribute."

"Give up the tribute! I don't see how that goes with the match."

"It goes altogether with it, and is part and parcel of it. King Sweyn offers to give up the tribute as Gunnhilda's morning gift."

"If that be so, I am all for the marriage," said King Burislaf, with the air of a man relieved of a great load of care. "It is everything to be good friends with these Danes, and not to have them always invading our borders. If King Sweyn marries your sister and gives up the tribute there is no reason why there should not be peace for ever between the Wends and Danes."

"Quite my view, father," said Astrida; "and when King Sweyn comes and is married—"

"What then?" asked Burislaf.

"Why then, I suppose, as Sigvald will have fulfilled both the conditions, that he will claim my hand, and I shall be married, too, and you will only have Geira left."

"I am afraid it must be so," said Burislaf. "We have given our word, and words at least even kings can keep. I am sorry for you, but so it must be. I could have wished you a more noble husband."

"I am quite content to take Sigvald as he is, father," said Astrida. "To my mind, the man who is bold enough and crafty enough to seize King Sweyn and bring him hither, is more worth having than all the Kings of the North."

"If you are happy, I am happy," said the easy Burislaf. "Besides, so long as you are Lady of Jomsburg, we shall not lose you altogether, while Denmark is far to see. But now that you have told me everything, let us go to breakfast. Nothing now remains but to tell Sigvald that he may bring King Sweyn hither as soon as ever he can."

But while Burislaf was making himself smart for his interview with Sigvald, Sigvald and Astrida had met, and she had told him all that had passed. Of course he did not enter into that lady's bower, which in those ages was in the case of unmarried women almost as sacred in the West as in the East; but love is just the same in all ages, and laughed at locksmiths, and parents and guardians just as heartily in the tenth century as he does in the nineteenth. Sigvald and Astrida met, therefore—where we cannot tell; but there was perfect intelligence between them, and in that assurance Sigvald went to breakfast with the Wendish King.

"We have thought over what you said last night," said Burislaf, with the most barefaced hypocrisy; "and we have well weighed your offer on the part of King Sweyn. Tell him that he is heartily welcome on Wendish soil, and that we are willing to make this match with our daughter Gunnhilda, if he will first consent to forego that claim to tribute which his father made."

"I will bear your message to the King," said

Sigvald; "and in two nights expect us back to the wedding feast."

"Two nights;" said King Burislaf, "that is but a short space. There are clothes to be made, not to speak of the ale and mead and meat that must be procured."

"King Sweyn bade me say," said Sigvald, "that he was eager to get home, as well he might be, seeing how he parted from his people. The Queen's waiting-women must stitch their fingers sore, and the King's thralls scour the country to bring in beeves and sheep; the King's huntsmen must search the forest, and his fishermen the rivers. There is good store of mead and ale in the cellars of the King, and besides all this there will be so much love at this banquet that all shortcomings will be forgotten. Your majesty will bear it in mind that as soon as I have brought King Sweyn hither and he has given up the tribute I am free to claim the Princess's hand, and be assured I mean to claim it."

"I will bear it in mind," said King Burislaf, graciously, "but remember you shall not have Astrida if Sweyn does not give up the tribute."

"I am quite ready to agree to that, and for that reason I beg your majesty to say nothing of the second marriage till King Sweyn has uttered his mind about the tribute; say nothing about me or Astrida till he has spoken out. As soon as that happens I will come forward and claim her hand."

"Be it so," said the King, and so those two parted. Sigvald took horse and rode off, and King Burislaf held long conferences with his Butler and Marshal, while Gangrel Speedifoot scoured the country to bring in stores of mead and ale and meat. How the Queen's waiting-women sewed and stitched and how the kitchen chimneys of the Grange smoked we forbear to tell. Suffice it to say, that when the evening of the second night came everything was ready for the bridal banquet.

During this time King Sweyn had sat moodily in Jomsburg considering his hard fate; snatched away from his realm and made to marry against his will, he was in no very good humour. Nothing that the Vikings could do gave him any pleasure; he showed no fear, but little joy, and it was a relief to him when he heard by the warder's horn that Sigvald had re-entered the burg.

But eager as he was to know the news it was quite beneath his royal position, and, indeed, beneath that of any free man in those days, to show any curiosity about his fate. He and Sigvald met therefore some time before the supper, at which all announcements were inevitably made; but they talked of the weather or the ships or the crops, or whatever was most indifferent.

But when the boards were cleared in the hal Sigvald rose up as before, drank the King's health with the usual formality, and passed the horn. Then the King drank to Sigvald and the Vikings, and while the mead went round waite for what Sigvald had to say.

As soon as the hum of toast-drinking had sub sided, Sigvald rose and said:

"I have now, King Sweyn, to tell you how m errand to King Burislaf has fared. I found hi well and the fair Gunnhilda well, and I did n fail to plead your suit for her hand with all th power that I could. The end of it all is, to mak a long story short, that King Burislaf is ready to give you his daughter on one condition."

Here he paused, and King Sweyn caught him up eagerly,

"And what is that?"

"His condition is an easy one," said Sigvald. "Easy for such a King as he to make, and easier still for such a mighty King as you to grant. In the early days of your father, Harold Bluetooth, there was, as we all know, and, indeed, you yourself have named it, some claim of a tax or tribute which your father said the Wends were bound to pay, and which the Wends refused."

Here King Sweyn, says the chronicler, turned as red as blood, and was swollen with wrath.

"I will never give up that tribute," he said, "which I have besides lately asked for; a King should never go back on his word."

"The King says," Sigvald went on, "he will never go back in his word. Some words are uttered to be given up, idle words, unreal claims, rights as some men call them, like this."

"I say it again," said Sweyn, "I will never go back on my word."

"Better that," said Sigvald fiercely, "than not to go back to Denmark."

"How so, Sigvald?" said Sweyn in the same tone; "Dost thou threaten me, thy liege Lord?"

"Liege Lord in Denmark, but equal to a king in Jomsburg," said Sigvald. "I make no threat. So long as you are with us, King Sweyn, we will treat you like a king, but then Jomsburg is not Denmark, nor is the yellow East Sea the blue Sound or Belt. Far pleasanter are the beechen woods of Schleswig and the islands than the fir forests of the Wends. Unless the King yields this little matter of the tribute he will have to stay long in Jomsburg, the winter over perhaps. Not to mention the loss of such a match and the third part of Wendland after Burislaf's death."

"How so?" said King Sweyn, "I never heard of that third part of Wendland."

"Because your majesty is so hasty," said Sigvald. "Had you waited I was coming to that. King Burislaf has no son nor male heir. After his death his three daughters will share his realm between them, and if Denmark get that third of Wendland which lies nearest to Denmark, that, methinks, would be worth ten times this tribute, which is only a claim after all and has never been paid."

"I never thought of that," said King Sweyn.

"It is a sad thing when men will not think," said Sigvald; "worst of all when kings who ought to think most think least, or not at all."

"I am willing to think over it," said the king.

"And not only to think of it but to do it," said Sigvald; "and, while I am about it, there is another thing that you might think of, and that is this, kings when they marry princesses of royal race and when that king is of great lineage are wont to give their brides on the morrow of the marriage a morning gift. What better morning gift could King Sweyn give to Gunnhilda, Burislaf's daughter, than this tribute which he claims? That would be indeed a royal way of giving up the tribute."

"I am willing to make the match on those terms," said King Sweyn, "so that in all things I am treated as a king, and not pushed aside into a corner by Burislaf."

"That you may rely on," said Sigvald; "I and three hundred of our bravest men will go with you to your wedding, and be your body guard, before two nights are out. All is settled and arranged, and when you have given up the tribute and have returned to Jomsburg with your queen, we Vikings of Jomsburg will speed you hence to Denmark with a squadron of thirty ships."

Then he went on :

"There is yet another thing too that you must think of. It will be more to your honour if your father-in-law is a king who pays tax and tribute to no man, so that in giving it up you will only increase your own grandeur, for those kings are surely greater who pay no tribute. For these and many other reasons you must see that this match, so far from being unequal, is one which will add to your glory and renown."

"You speak so forcibly and with such persuasion, Sigvald," said Sweyn, "that I say outright that this match is much to my mind, and now I again say let us think no more of it to-night. Ho! butler, fill up my horn with mead."

So King Sweyn and the Vikings spent that night in wassail and revelry, and when they went to bed there was scarce one of them that did not stagger, except Beorn, the Welshman.

"Whatever I have said of Sigvald and his breaking the law," he said to himself, "I must own that no man is his match in wit. Think of carrying King Sweyn off and making him marry Burislaf's daughter, and all that Sigvald may wed the fair Astrida. It is a mad world, so it has been and so it will be. Women with their pretty faces turn it upside down. I thank all the gods that no woman cares to marry me, just as I care to marry no woman."

With which sage reflections the veteran lay down, turned over on his side, and was soon sound asleep.

CHAPTER XV.

HOW KING SWEYN AND SIGVALD WERE MARRIED.

Two days after, as they had promised, King Sweyn rode out of Jomsburg with Sigvald and Thorkell the Tall by his side and three hundred Vikings at his back. Never had such a gallant band of horsemen been seen in Wendland.

As the night began to fall they came to Burislaf's grange, and the flutter which their arrival caused at that court may be better imagined than described.

As for Burislaf himself he was already seated in his high seat in the hall, a position which so well became him. To tell the truth he and his whole household were rather alarmed at the prospect of entertaining the hereditary foe of their house, even when he came as a friend. They had caged the lion and were afraid to look at him.

The queen and the princesses, too, were in

the hall on the cross-bench on the dais, the two brides with wimples over their heads and long veils which quite concealed their features.

Whether Gunnhilda shed tears at the prospect of leaving her home we cannot say, but we are sure that though Astrida's heart beat high she shed no tears.

The King's chiefs were on his side of the hall, one hundred in number, and room was left for King Sweyn and as many of his Vikings opposite. The rest of the three hundred were feasted with men of equal rank among the Wends.

As for the butler and the marshal, they received the King, led him to a room by himself, held fine linen for him to wipe his hands and face, and brought him warm water in a silver basin.

When all was ready the warders sounded their horns, all the hounds bayed and barked, the steeds snorted and neighed in their stalls, and all the world around Burislaf's grange knew that the mighty King Sweyn was on his way to his wedding feast.

Into the hall strode the moody King, followed

closely by Sigvald and the rest of the Viking chiefs, of whom only Bui again had remained to keep order and rule in Jomsburg. Before him went the marshal and the butler.

When he had gone so far as half-way up the hall opposite to the King's high seat, Burislaf rose, and without moving from his high seat, said, in a loud voice—

"Welcome, King Sweyn, on Wendish land! Welcome to your bridal feast!"

Without bowing, Sweyn replied—

"Hail, Burislaf, King of the Wends. Right glad am I to find myself under your roof."

"Take your seat opposite, you and your men," said Burislaf, "and eat and drink and be merry. When your hunger and thirst are over we will speak of the wedding."

So the two kings sat and feasted, and the banquet was like any other banquet in those days, except that more meat was consumed and more mead drank in a given period of time than the butler and the marshal had ever heard of or seen before.

When all this eating and drinking was over, the boards were cleared and removed by the thralls, and the real business of the evening began.

Then Sigvald, who sat next to King Sweyn on his right, rose and said—

"It is well known to you, King Burislaf, and to you also, King Sweyn, why we are all here. King Sweyn has heard, as we all have heard, of the beauty of the Princess Gunnhilda. It is not good for a man, least of all for a king, to be without a wife, and so he has turned his eyes where good women are to be found. This is why he has come so far from his own land to seek a wife in Wendland, and it is another mark of respect to you, King Burislaf, that instead of making his bridal feast in Denmark and having the bride brought to him, he has come to your grange to keep this feast here, and then to bring her home himself. For these three days, King Burislaf, the Princess Gunnhilda has been betrothed to King Sweyn; and though the courtship has been short, there is an old saw which says, 'the sooner the better for a good thing.' How say you, then, King Burislaf, shall my liege lord in Denmark, King Sweyn here, have your daughter Gunnhilda to wife?"

"What dower will King Sweyn give my daughter?" said Burislaf, "and what shall be her morning gift?"

"She shall have Moen, and Falster, and Langeland, and a third of the King's dues at Oresund for her dower," answered Sigvald; "and for her morning gift King Sweyn will behave right nobly; but for that matter I would rather he spoke for himself."

"How say you, King Sweyn?" said Burislaf; "shall my daughter, if she marries you, have all these islands and dues for her dower, and will you take her to wife by the most binding rites which you Danes respect?"

"I am ready," said King Sweyn, "to take her as my wife, and to grant her those islands and dues as her dower, and to wed her with Thor's holy hammer, the rite in which we Danes still put most faith, for our Christianity is as young as yours. But if I do all this, what shall Gunnhilda have as her portion?"

"That," said Burislaf, "is soon answered. The line of my father has ended on the spindle-side. I have no male heir, no son, no brother, no uncle, and according to our laws, when I die my three daughters will share my kingdom between them. Gunnhilda's portion will be a third of all Wendland. Is that enough?"

"It is," said Sweyn; "and on these terms I am willing to make the match."

"But one thing is still unsaid," said Burislaf; "the morning gift, which by our customs the bride must have. Whether you have it or no, we must have it, for without it no marriage is binding on the Wends. How say you, then, as to the morning gift, King Sweyn?"

"We have an old saw which says," replied King Sweyn, "that there is always a short cut to the house of a good friend. I little thought when I left Denmark so suddenly that I should take this long journey, least of all that I should so soon find myself friends with thee, King Burislaf. But so it has been. This long way has proved a short cut to friendship; and though there has been sometimes enmity between our houses and our folk, I am ready to forget and forgive all those former feuds. My father, Harold Bluetooth, as is well known, claimed tribute from the Wends, and there are some here at least who know that it is not so long ago since I thought of demanding it. I think between father-in-law and son-in-law there should neither be tax nor tribute, and that the son-in-law is a grander man if his father-in-law is free from all tribute. At the same time, there is the claim. What I will do, therefore, King Burislaf, in the matter of that morning gift of which you have spoken is to declare here in the presence of all these witnesses, my men and yours, that as soon as I am wedded to Gunnhilda I will give up all and every claim to tribute from the Wends."

A roar of applause followed from what may be called the Wendish side of the house. To tell the truth, the Wends knew they were no match for the Danes in fight, and every man just as much as King Burislaf blessed the happy chance which had brought King Sweyn to seek a wife among the Wends, and to give up the tax which not a month before King Sweyn had demanded so insultingly.

"The King gives up the tribute!" "No tribute to the Danes!" rang round the hall, and the excitement was intense.

"That I think is a right royal morning gift,"

said King Burislaf, when order was restored. "I think before we proceed further, as talking is dry work, we had better have a horn of mead in memory of King Sweyn's gracious words."

Round went the horns, and they were speedily drained, amidst shouts of "Long live King Sweyn!" "No tribute to the Danes!" and nothing could now seem fairer than the prospects of the feast.

When the uproar died away King Burislaf rose again and said—

"As all that is needful has thus been settled by word of mouth in the sight and hearing of many witnesses, we will now proceed to the wedding. Yonder sits the bride on the cross-bench. May it please you, King Sweyn, to hallow the bride."

Then a procession was formed, in which the marshal went first and the taper-bearers, then came King Burislaf, then King Sweyn, then Sigvald, playing the part of best man, then Thorkell the Tall, and so on, Wends and Vikings in double file in the order of their rank.

Thrice they walked round the hall, and on the third round halted before the daïs on which sat the Queen and the Princesses on the cross-bench.

Here a difficulty occurred, for there sat two brides both closely veiled, and both dressed alike in virgin white. Hitherto they had escaped Sweyn's notice. As they caught his eye he turned and said, half out loud, to Sigvald—

"Be there two brides, or do I see double? though we have drank no mead to speak of."

"There are two brides," said Sigvald. "That will be made clear presently. Gunnhilda is she that sits on the right hand of the Queen in the place of honour."

Then Burislaf called to the Marshal: "Where is the holy hammer?—produce it."

Then the Marshal drew forth from his robes, or what passed muster for robes, an ancient axe of flint, one of those stone implements which we call celts, but which were then supposed to be the thunderbolts of Thor, and tokens of his maul with which he smashed the skulls of the giants.

"This rite," said Burislaf, turning to King Sweyn, "is common to both our races. In these days we know not what we worship, for as you well said, Christianity is young in the North. And so the old form lingers, though few still believe in the ancient gods. Whether it be Peran or Thor, both Danes and Wends worshipped the same God of Thunder under two names. Hallow the bride, therefore, with the Holy Maul, and so take Gunnhilda to thyself for thy lawful wife."

King Sweyn took the flint axe, and stepping up to the veiled figure on the right of the Queen, laid it on the lap of the bride, and then called out in a loud voice—

"With this Holy Maul, I, Sweyn, King of Denmark, take thee, Gunnhilda, Burislaf's daughter, to be my wedded wife."

As he said this the warders blew their horns, and the harpers struck up their wild minstrelsy, of which the reader has already heard. When the savage melody died away King Burislaf called out—

"Now are Sweyn, Harold's son, King of Denmark, and Gunnhilda, Burislaf's daughter, Princess of the Wends, man and wife."

Thunders of applause followed this announcement, in the course of which the Marshal removed the Holy Maul from the bride's lap, and held it in his hand, as if ready for further use.

All this time the bride sat motionless, and made no sign. Her part in the ceremony was purely passive. In this way brides were, as it was called in old times just as much as in modern, "given away" by their fathers. In the earliest times brides were stolen from their homes and carried off like captives by suitors. Next they were sold by their fathers, and then given away. In modern times they are as often sold as given away, but it is the fashion to call that a gift which in reality is too often a sale.

As the ritualistic part of the ceremony was over, and what was called the bride's feast was about to begin, King Sweyn turned to go back to his seat, but Burislaf touched him and said:

"Bide a while, King Sweyn, we have still to wed the second bride."

"One bride is enough at a time for any man," said King Sweyn, whose wits at this period of the evening were anything but clear. "I cannot marry both your daughters."

"It is not needed," said Burislaf, with a

chuckle. "We have already found a bridegroom for our eldest daughter."

"I see no other bridegroom," said King Sweyn.

"And yet he stands by you, shoulder to shoulder," said Burislaf.

King Sweyn turned again, and saw to his amazement Sigvald in the act of reaching out his hand to the Marshal to take the Holy Maul.

"Sigvald the bridegroom!" he exclaimed. "I never heard of it. He keeps his counsel close. Is there guile under this also?"

"There is no guile," King Sweyn, said Burislaf. Astrida and Sigvald have been betrothed, so to speak, much longer than Gunnhilda and yourself."

"I do not understand it," said Sweyn.

"Hush!" said Burislaf. "Do not break the bride's peace. See, he lays the Holy Maul on her lap, and hallows her as his wedded wife!"

"I see it all," said Sweyn, "but I do not understand it;" but his words were lost in the shouts of applause with which the Vikings and

Wends alike answered Burislaf's second announcement.

"Now are Sigvald, Harold's son, Captain of Jomsburg, and Astrida, Burislaf's daughter, Princess of the Wends, man and wife."

Then followed the brides' feast, as it was called, a mere form, in which they still sat on the cross bench, and were served with meat and drink, which they could but taste under their long veils, while the men looked on, and the minstrels played. As soon as it was over, they, with the rest of the women, retired for the night to the women's apartments, first paying the "bride's fee" to the Marshal, and their waiting women for their attendance at the ceremony. The bridegrooms saw no more of their brides that night, for, according to the old usage, though lawfully wedded, they were not "bedded," as the phrase was, till the bridal or bride's ride had taken place, in which, when the marriage was celebrated out of his own house, the bridegroom brought his bride solemnly home. On this occasion the home of both the bridegrooms was taken to be the Castle of Jomsburg.

After the women had departed, the men still kept up the feast till far on into the night ; and it seemed to Burislaf's butler that the end of the world, so far as quaffing mead was concerned, had surely come. Even King Sweyn seemed to have recovered his surprise at hearing there was a second bridegroom, and that Sigvald, in the hall. No doubt he felt as eager as the giant in the Edda to lift the bride's veil, and see what she was like ; but even he was restrained by the manners of the time, and whatever curiosity he felt, kept it all to himself.

All things must have an end, and so had this wedding feast. What Burislaf was to do during the winter with his empty cellar and larder, literally eaten out of house and home, does not concern us. Suffice it to say, that he had married both his daughters, one of them to a king, and another to a man who had proved himself the boldest and most skilful warrior of his time. He had, besides, struck up a friendship with Sweyn, got rid of the tribute, and was no longer plagued with periodical fears of a Danish invasion. As he lay down to rest, he might well chuckle and congratulate himself on his good fortune in having such a friend as Sigvald. Nor had Sigvald cause to complain. He had changed the law at Jomsburg with little trouble, married the woman of his choice, and done that deed in carrying off King Sweyn, and bringing him to King Burislaf, which would for ever make his name famous in the North. What more could he wish, except that King Sweyn might not envy him the possession of Astrida, and might not know all the circumstances which had led to his captivity. What Sweyn thought is unknown. After all his mead he slept, no doubt, sound and well.

CHAPTER XVI.

THE RIDE TO JOMSBURG.

NEXT morning every one was up betimes. After the morning meal the brides were to be given away by King Burislaf to their husbands, and then they were to mount and ride for Jomsburg.

When King Sweyn and Sigvald met, it was plain to see that there was some coolness between them. Never, even on the morning after he had been carried off, had the King seemed so ill at ease. Sigvald, on his part, had something plainly on his mind.

"They stare at one another like two bears in a pitfall, Vagn," said Beorn. "Were not Sweyn so completely in our power, they would soon come to blows."

Sweyn, like kings in all times, had little to do on such an occasion. Had he been a king now-a-days, in all probability he would have smoked, and so consoled himself; but as there was then no such resource, he loitered about, and did nothing till breakfast, while Sigvald was busy looking after his horses, and getting all things ready for their long ride.

At last the morning meal came, and with it the critical moment when the bridegrooms were to see the brides unveiled. Unless a man in those times had seen his intended before the wedding day, he was in the position, as Beorn the Welchman irreverently remarked, of a man buying a pig in a poke. He might be bound for ever to the ugliest and loathliest woman in the world, and in that plight was King Sweyn.

Now it could not be denied that Gunnhilda was a pretty girl, only she was not so pretty as Astrida, who was really beautiful. She was tall, and dark, and majestic as her mother, while Gunnhilda was simply a pretty likeness of her short and squat sire. She would have passed muster well enough had Astrida been away; but there Astrida was, and there was no denying her superior charms. Added to this, Gunnhilda was believed in the family to be as stupid as Astrida was wise.

When King Burislaf saw King Sweyn loitering about the court-yard in that listless way, he went up to him without ceremony, and hoped he had slept well, just for all the world like a courteous prince of the present century. We say courteous, because there are some kings, alas! even in this century, though not English ones, whose manners and address are anything but courteous.

"Though not like Freyr," said Sweyn, "who could not sleep for nights and nights till he had got Gerda to wife, I may still say that I have been awake long before dawn. I am eager, to tell you the truth, to see the bride, and to acknowledge the beauty of my queen."

"The morning meal will be served at once," said Burislaf, "and then your majesty will have your heart's desire."

When he had said that, he turned away, and said to himself:

"I wonder what he will think of her when he sees her?"

"The morning meal is served," cried the butler; and the two Kings and the Vikings, every man of whom was as sharp set as though they had never put morsel into their mouths, streamed into the hall.

"If King Sweyn were hungry," says the chronicler, "his eyes were hungrier still to behold his bride, of whose loveliness Sigvald had told him so much, all which he had taken on trust."

His first care, therefore, was to look towards the cross-bench, where the Queen, and the princesses, or brides, now sat in the light of day without wimple or veil of any kind. The evening before, still as death, they were now as lively as larks, and chatted to one another as only sisters can.

While Sweyn was watching them, and taking the measure of their charms, others in the hall were watching him.

"Mark his face, boy," said Beorn to Vagn; "he grows as red as blood, like all that family. Other men turn white; but the Knytlings always show their wrath by a red face and a swollen look. See, he swells as if his kirtle could not hold him. Take my word for it, he feels that he has been cheated in this wedding by the Captain, who picked out the fairest maiden for himself, and left the less fair for him, the King."

"He may feel wrathful," said Vagn, "but he dare not show it in words. He is quite in our power."

"True; but for all that, I am much mistaken if he does not show it in words ere we leave Burislaf's house."

"So the meal went on as all morning meals, only it was more ample. When it came to an end the horses were ready, and nothing remained to Burislaf but to give his daughters solemnly away, to lead them out of the house, as it was called, and to hand them over to their husbands.

"May it please you, King Sweyn," he said, "and you, Sigvald, Harold's son, to approach the daïs, and look upon your brides?"

Up rose King Sweyn without a word. When he reached the daïs, he stared savagely at both the princesses, and glared in anger, saying never a word.

"Say, King Sweyn, is the Queen fair to look on?" said Burislaf, who, perhaps, thought that Gunnhilda, being like himself, must be more beautiful than Astrida.

"Fair is the maiden," said Sweyn, swallowing down his wrath; "fair enough, were it not that a fairer than she sits by her!"

Then, turning to Sigvald, he said in a way most shocking for a king, a bridegroom, and a lover:

"Why told you me not, Sigvald, Harold's son, that Astrida was the fairer of the two?"

"Because, King Sweyn," said Sigvald, proudly, "because Gunnhilda was then the fairest of King Burislaf's unpledged daughters when I wooed her in your name. Long before that, Astrida was betrothed to me; and when a woman is once betrothed, King Sweyn, you know she is not free to become the choice of any other man."

"And pray," said King Sweyn, whose blood seemed now up, "pray what morning gift are you, Sigvald, Harold's son, to give to Astrida for giving herself over, and all her charms, to you?"

This question seemed to take Sigvald unawares, and he paused for a reply; but, to the amazement of all, his bride came to his relief.

"King Sweyn, Harold's son," said Astrida, haughtily, "asks what morning gift Sigvald is to give to me, his wife. Let me tell you, King, this is one of those gifts which has been paid beforehand: Sigvald has given it me already."

"And pray what was it?" said King Sweyn, moodily.

"I am ready to utter it; and all the more, because it concerns yourself, King Sweyn," said Astrida. "Sigvald, Harold's son, paid me my morning gift when he seized you, and carried you off from Denmark, and brought you here, and married you to my sister, who is too good for a king who was so worsted in a struggle of wit and daring. Besides all that, it would have been quite gift enough for me had he only forced you, as he has, to forego all claim to tribute on the Wends."

"So those were the conditions," said King Sweyn, with the air of a man who at last felt all the humiliation of his position.

"They were, King Sweyn," said Sigvald, "All that I was to do to win Astrida's hand; and, against all hope, I have done it, I alone. You would never have heard these things, lord, unless you had asked questions. But as you have asked them, you have had your answer.

Now answer another, which I am forced to put to you, King Sweyn. Will you take Gunnhilda, and treat her in every way as your queen, on your word as a king, and go back to Denmark straightway with all honour? or, will you give her up, and stay here in King Burislaf's hands, or come back with us to Jomsburg, and stay there with us, and not go back at all to Denmark?"

"A plain question," said King Sweyn, "and it shall be as plainly answered. No one can strive against superior force. I will treat Gunnhilda as becomes a queen in every way, and I will go back to Denmark. Now let us ride to Jomsburg as soon as may be."

All this time King Burislaf had stood by as speechless as his queen, while every man in the hall looked on and listened. When Sweyn had uttered these last words, the Wendish king stepped forward, and said:

"We have heard from Astrida's lips the morning gift which Sigvald has paid her. But we have not heard yours in proper form. We know since last night what it is to be, but now deign to utter it?"

Thus challenged, King Sweyn looked fiercely at King Burislaf, and said:

"About this there is a long story, deign to hear it, King Burislaf. Once on a time there was a folk of eagles, and hard by their land dwelt a a folk of tits. The tits were small, and of no repute; they lived on dirt and filth, while the eagles lived on the fish of the sea, and the fowl of the air, and the beasts of the field. But all at once the tits went to war with the eagles in their pride, and crossed the border; but they could not do much harm, they were so small. For all that the eagles were angry, and crossed the border into the tits' land, and wasted it, but they could not live on dirt as the tits lived, nor could they catch the tits, they were so small, and flew so fast. So they retired to their own land, and said: 'This land is nothing worth, and the tits are poor and wretched. Just to say that we have been here, we will make the tits pay tribute, though they have nothing to pay it with.' So it went on for years and years, the eagles claiming, and the tits never paying tribute. At last there came one eagle fleeter than the rest, whose wings were stronger and longer, and he said: 'I will make these tits pay tribute,' so he sent a message to the tit-king, and said: 'Pay me that tribute, or I will destroy thee.' But the tits sent no tribute. It so happened that the tit-king had a friend, called the Fox, and they took counsel together, and the fox said: 'If I bring thee the king of the eagles prisoner, wilt thou give me thy daughter to wife.' To that the tit-king said: 'Aye.' So the fox went craftily, as only foxes can go, and found the king of the eagles asleep, and carried him off to tit-land, and showed him to the tit-king, and said: 'Marry the tit-king's daughter, or spend your life for ever in a cage, and give up the tribute which the tits have never paid.' So the king of the eagles said: 'What good can come of a match when one mate is an eagle and the other a tit? All the same, sooner than live all my life in a cage, I will marry the tit-princess.' So he married her, and was set free, and gave up the tax and returned to his own land. That is the story of the eagle-king and the tit-king, King Burislaf, and I say, like the eagle-king, 'though my wings are long and strong, they are of no use to me unless I am free to fly whither I will, and so I marry your daughter, and give up the tribute to her as her morning gift; but whether the eagle-king and the tit-princess live together long and happily is more than I can tell, for when birds are ill-mated they do not thrive, and it is an old saw, 'that birds of a feather flock most together,' and so no doubt it has been with you and Sigvald."

"Let us not prolong the war of words," said Burislaf. "You came hither in peace, King Sweyn, and in peace you shall return. It is true that Sigvald has wrought all that Astrida said; but Gunnhilda and Geira were the only two of my daughters left, for Astrida was as good as given to Sigvald before you ever set foot in Jomsburg. As for eagles and tits, I know not what you mean. We Wends have often held our own against you Danes, and so we will again. It is not so long since the Danish eagle flew like a tit before the army of the Emperor Otho, who is an eagle indeed. But, as I have said, let there be an end of this. Go in peace, and take Gunnhilda with you. She will make you a good wife; and, as for Sigvald, though you are his liege-lord in Denmark, here, on Wendish soil, he is your equal, and in every way worthy to be the brother-in-law of the King of Denmark."

With these words, he took his daughters by their right and left hands, leading them out of the hall in that way. As they passed the door-sill, he turned and said to Sweyn and Sigvald, who followed close behind :

" With these hands I lead my daughters out of the house, that I may give them to thee, Sweyn, Harold's son, King of Denmark, and to thee, Sigvald, Harold's son, Captain of Jomsburg. Take them, and be good to them, as they will be bonny and buxom to both of you, and now may all the gods, both the old and the new, speed you and them on your way."

Then Sweyn and Sigvald each took their wife's right hand in theirs, and, leading them to their palfreys, put them up into the saddle, each saying as he did so :

" Now are you, Gunnhilda, and now are you, Astrida, my lawful wife, and no other."

Next all the Vikings mounted, and Burislaf and his chiefs mounted too, and they rode off as hard as they could on their bridal procession to Jomsburg.

Half way between Burislaf's Grange and the Burg, King Burislaf turned and rode back with his men, but the rest rode on ever faster and faster till they neared Jomsburg, when the ride became a race between the two bridegrooms and their brides, which could first pass the gate into the Vikings' stronghold.

Here, too, fortune was against King Sweyn and for Sigvald. The Viking Captain distanced the King in the race, but men marked it as a token that Sigvald himself was beaten by Astrida, who at the last moment pressed her palfrey on, and just got through the gate before him.

"Sigvald for this once rules the roost over Sweyn," said Beorn to Vagn; "but the end of this race is a sign that Astrida will rule over Sigvald, crafty and deep withal though he be. Depend on it, in this case, too, the grey mare will be the better horse."

That night, again, there was a great feast in the Vikings' hall, and the King and Sigvald sat over against one another in their high seats, the King still keeping the seat of honour. Side by side with them sat Gunnhilda and Astrida, and it was remarked that King Sweyn, having vented his wrath, was in a better temper at night than he had been in the morning. Whether it was that the black cloud had passed away, or that he thought it best to be on his good behaviour so long as he was still in the Vikings' power, certain it is that he was gentle and gracious, and spoke as kindly to his Queen at meat, as though she had been the true choice of his heart.

When the meal was over, Sigvald rose, and said :

"I have now accomplished all that I have undertaken to do. Betrothed and married King Sweyn to a fair princess of one of the best houses in the North, and at the same time set the Wends free from tribute, and so made King Burislaf a mightier man, and a better father-in-law to both of us. It is true also that I have got a fair princess for my own wife, the very sight of whom will prove to this gallant company how good a thing it was to do away our law against marriage. What I have now to say, is to ask King Sweyn to remember our former friendship, to forget any cause of quarrel which we may lately have given him, and to feel sure that every man of this company would be willing to follow him to the death. I now call on you all to drink to the health of King Sweyn and Queen Gunnhilda, and to wish them a safe and speedy voyage to their kingdom."

With a great uproar the horns were drained, and when it died away, King Sweyn rose, and said:

"I cannot say that there have not happened things lately which have made me rather look to the new hatred than to the old love which was between me and Sigvald. Perhaps Sigvald may have thought that so long as his father Strut-Harold lived I held pledges of his in my hand, and even now he may believe that I would revenge on the sire the wrongs I have suffered from the son. But this, I speak it out before you all, is not at all to my mind. I should think myself a niddering and a dastard if I touched a hair of Strut-Harold's head. For the sake of future friendship, and in honour of this gallant band, whose life is but that which my own once was, I am willing to let bygones be bygones, and to part as much a friend of Sigvald's as I ever was. The day may come when he will have to drink Strut-Harold's funeral ale, just as you noble Bui will have to drink it after Veseti in Bornholm. Then, perhaps, it might seem that I should have as strong a hold on Sigvald on my native soil as he has now on me in this foreign land. But I only speak of this to say beforehand that whatever happens, Sigvald and you Vikings are as free to come to Denmark, and to have an asylum there as you ever were, always on the understanding that you do not waste my goods or spoil my subjects."

Here a murmur of applause interrupted the King, who called for a horn of mead; and, holding it out at arm's length, called out:

"I drink to the health of Sigvald, Harold's son, and of Astrida, the lady of Jomsburg."

This toast was received with rapturous applause, and it was evident that the King had won back all his old favour with the Vikings.

All now went smoothly, Sigvald was merry and cheerful. King Sweyn was no longer dull or moody, and the feast was complete when an Icelandic skald came forward, and asked to be allowed to sing THE SONG OF FRITHIOF.

"Which of the songs of Frithiof?" asked the King.

"His Viking Code, lord," said the skald.

"When one lives with the wolves, one must howl with them," said the King. "Besides, I am an old Viking myself. Let us hear the song."

Then the skald stood before the King's high-seat, and calling out "This is the Viking Code of Frithiof Hilding's son when he took to sea-roving," sung these verses:

"As he hovered about as a hawk on the wing, and oër sea-
wastes his war-galleys rode,
For his champions on board he wrote statutes and laws;
now list to his sea-roving code.

Throw no awning oër ship, never slumber in house, within
doors stand an enemy's crew,
On his shield sword in hand let a Viking take rest; let
his awning be heaven, the blue.

Short haft hath the hammer of conquering Thor, but an
ell long the sword that Frey swayed;
'Tis enough; hast thou heart, stand up close to thy foe,
and too short will not then be thy blade.

When the wind bloweth high hoist thy sail to the top,
'tis merry in storm not to flinch;
Keep her full! Keep her full! none but cowards strike
sail, sooner founder than take in an inch.

Maids are safe upon shore, they may not come on board,
were she Freyja, of maiden beware ;
For that dimple on cheek is a pitfall for thee, and those
fair flowing tresses a snare.

Wine is Valfather's drink, and a bout is allowed; if thy
head thou canst keep, never fear;
Whoso stumbles on land can stand up, but to Ran, to the
slumberous, stumblest thou here.

If a chapman sail by, his ship thou shalt shield, but the
weak must not tribute withhold;
Thou art lord of thy wave, he is slave of his wares, and thy
steel is as good as his gold.

Now foemen are sighted, now strife comes and blows,
under shield now the warm blood is spilt;
If thou yieldest one step, take thy leave of our band, 'tis
the law, and so do as thou wilt.

Wounds are Vikings' delight, and they set off their man,
on forehead and bosom when shown;
Let them bleed! never bind them till day comes again,
not sooner, wilt thou be our own."

The skald's song was received by the company with roars of applause. When it was over, the King rewarded the singer with a ring of gold which he took off his arm, saying, as he did so, "This take in remembrance of the days when I too roved the sea-wastes like Frithiof the bold."

"A right good song, foster-child," cried old Beorn, "that I call a true Viking Code; no houses, no women, no marriage, but ever roving, ever fighting, ever spoiling, ever drinking until death."

It was now late, the pine-torches were extinguished, the log fires burned low, and everything gave token that it was time to retire for the night.

The Queen and the Princess had taken their departure even before the Icelander had delivered his song. They and their waiting-women found their way to the lodgings provided for the King and Queen and for Sigvald and his wife.

The rest now followed, and so ended the day which gave Denmark and King Sweyn a Queen and brought women first into Jomsburg.

Nothing is recorded of the appearance of the wedded couples next morning, but if King Sweyn were but half as happy with his Queen as Astrida was with Sigvald, he might well have been considered as happy indeed.

CHAPTER XVII.

KING SWEYN RETURNS TO DENMARK.

It was not to be expected that King Sweyn would not wish to return to Denmark as soon as ever he could get free; nor was there any longer an excuse for keeping him in Jomsburg. The season was growing short, and the late September nights were at hand, when it was supposed that the seas grew unsafe.

Those were the days when little time was lost in deliberation. Two days after his return with his bride, King Sweyn was ready to depart. As they had promised, Sigvald and the Vikings prepared to see him home, with a squadron of thirty ships, and altogether his homeward voyage promised, as it well might, to be much more glorious than that which brought him to Jomsburg.

The only person to be pitied was Gunnhilda, who was now about to be trusted to the tender mercies of the reclaimed Viking, who was now King of Denmark.

Many and long were the conversations of the sisters before they parted, and the superior sense and wit of Astrida greatly helped to cheer up her melancholy sister, who, to take her own view of the case, felt very much as though she were about to embark on the adventurous voyage of matrimony with a Danish Bluebeard. Princesses talked in those days very much as they talk now, and Gunnhilda's words of complaint, translated into modern language, ran thus :

"I am sure I shall never endure it ; I am sure I shall be worn and worried to death ; I am sure Sweyn will be a brute of a husband."

So she went on with much more of the same sort, to all of which Astrida only answered :

"No, no, I am sure he will not ; I can see he is getting fonder and fonder of you every day. If you are unhappy it will be all your own fault. If Sweyn were my husband I could rule him with a feather."

"I am sure I wish he were," said Gunnhilda. "If you think he will make so good a husband why not change; you would rule Sweyn, and then you would soon rule Denmark."

"I would not change if I could," said Astrida, "Sigvald is more to me than if he were twenty times King of Denmark."

"That is just it," said Gunnhilda, "you are fond and proud of Sigvald, and he is fond and proud of you. Yours, though it did not begin so, ended in being a love-match, while mine was one of necessity and force."

"So royal matches always are, my dear," said Astrida. "One cannot be a Queen without smarting for it in some way."

"It seems as if I should smart for it in every way," said Gunnhilda.

"Not at all," said her sister. "Just think of it. You will go home to Denmark, and have ladies in your train, and see many new faces, all smiling, and all willing to do you service. Here I stay as yet the only lady in Jomsburg, with a tire-woman or two to wait on me. Would you not find that lonely."

"Now I think of it," said Gunnhilda, "it would be very dull here, and perhaps I might be better off in Denmark; but why did we ever leave home, where we were so happy? How I envy Geira in our father's grange."

"No doubt she too finds it dull without us and envies us our lot. And what does it all come to, but that no one thinks she is half as happy as she ought to be, and so no one is quite so happy as she might be. Now do try to make the best of it, and rely on it you will find being a Queen in Denmark not such a dreadful thing, after all."

"I will try," said Gunnhilda, and so the sisters said no more about it.

The morning of the third day came, and the thirty ships of the Vikings, which were to escort King Sweyn, were ready for sea. Thirty long-ships of fifty oars, each manned by one hundred sturdy sailors, lay alongside the wharves in the harbour.

As a little while ago we reckoned the strength of our ships by the number of their guns, so in those days ships were counted more or less powerful for the oars with which they were propelled. In the tenth century, a ship of fifty oars was considered large, and of the one hundred men which composed the crew, fifty rowed in what we should call "watches," or spells, while fifty remained idle till their time came to relieve them. These war-ships, or long-ships as they were called, were not unlike the galleys of the Barbary rovers in more modern times. They were hardly seaworthy in a heavy swell, such for instance as the large rollers which are sometimes met between Norway and Iceland; but in the narrow seas in the Baltic, and even in the North Sea between England and Denmark, they were the fighting-ships of the time; and in them, when the Crusades began, the Kings and Earls of the North and West skirted the German and French and Spanish coasts, till passing into the Mediterranean by the Gut of Gibraltar, they found themselves in waters exactly suited to their craft.

They were high out of the water at stern and stem, and the prow and cutwater were often carved into a figure-head in the form of a dragon, while the stern, the tiller, and rudder, took the shape of its coils and tail. We have already seen that in the stern under the poop was the captain's cabin. In the bow under a raised deck, which exactly corresponds to our forecastle, was the sleeping place of some of the crew. All round the undecked part amidships ran a gangway, on which, in action, the fighting men stood, and the gunwale, in the waist of the ship, was heightened in action by a bulwark, on the top of which was a rail on which the shields of the crew were hung till they were wanted. While they were in harbour, or when they lay up for the night, the undecked portion of the ship was covered by an awning, under which the rest of the crew slept.

For the rest, these ships had a single mast, and a large lug sail, with a foresail at the bow, but they chiefly relied on their oars for speed, and fifty stout rowers sent the long craft along at great speed.

It need scarcely be said that great Kings and Earls, and such captains as those of the Vikings, took great pains with their ships. They were gaily painted and gilded at stem and stern; their sails were sometimes red and blue and green in stripes; their vanes and weather-cocks and figure-heads were carved and gilded, and in a word a war-ship of that period was a sight to see, and literally "walked the waters like a thing of life."

Let us add that besides bows and arrows and spears and boat-hooks, with which the struggle with foemen was carried on, each ship brought with it into action a good store of stones, the rude artillery of the time, which, hurled by the stalwart arms of the crew, proved missiles fraught with wounds and death to those on whom they fell with full force.

Such and so armed were the thirty ships of the Vikings which formed the squadron of honour which was to escort King Sweyn and his consort to the Danish shore.

First and foremost among them was Sigvald's own ship, which bore what might be called the Admiral's flag. Then came the war-drake of Thorkell the Tall; then Bui's, the son of Veseti, whose boatswain bore at early dawn those two famous chests of gold down to the wharf. Next in order was the Snake, as she was called, of Vagn, Aki's son, one of the trimmest and fleetest of ships, and after her followed the galley of Beorn, the Welshman, higher out of the water than any of the rest, for she had been built to face the waves of the Irish Channel, and the North Sea, and not so gay, but perhaps more serviceable in a sea-fight than any of the others.

These were the ships of the leaders, the others were made up by the ships of captains of lesser note; but there was not one of them which could not hold her own against any vessel that was likely to meet them in those seas.

The night before the King sailed, the Vikings made him a great banquet, the details of which we spare the reader. Suffice it to say that it was a great and glorious feast, and that the Queen and her sister, who on this occasion had gone back to the true place of women on the cross-bench, were both merry and happy, while King Sweyn was brimful of joy at the prospect of his deliverance, and was proportionately gracious to Sigvald and his captains.

At last the hour of departure came. Down the King and Queen walked to Sigvald's ship, between a double line of Vikings drawn up on either side to do them honour. Then followed Sigvald and his captains. When all had stepped on board, the gangways to the shore were drawn on board. Each ship in order was towed out of the harbour by hawsers, made fast to the arch above. As Sigvald's ship felt the waves, the King took the tiller, for in those times Kings and Earls and mighty chiefs steered their own ships; the rowers fell lustily to their oars, the warders on the arch sounded their horns, the crews cheered, and those cheers were re-echoed by the thousands of the band who were left behind. As the war-ships bounded over the waters of the Baltic, King Sweyn exulted as he felt that he would be soon a King indeed again, and that each stroke of the rowers brought him nearer to the end of his captivity.

One thing, however, we have forgotten to say. Astrida went with Sigvald, and they were now as inseparable as Bui and his gold chests. She had an excuse, too, in departing from the custom of the age, which kept women at home while their husbands went to sea. She wished to see the last of her sister, and only went, she said, with a pardonable hypocrisy, to help to keep up the poor thing's spirits.

Were they sea-sick, those ladies? We should say certainly not, though we are not sure of the fact. Perhaps the sea was too smooth, perhaps Gunnhilda was too frightened, and Astrida too happy to be ill. They were inland ladies, it was true, who had scarcely ever seen the sea in their lives, so that was against them. We leave, therefore, the question as we found it, in the conviction that if those ladies were sea-sick for the first time they must have felt most miserable.

"It did not take long—twenty-four hours, it may be—to run a ship from Jomsburg to what is now Swedish, but was then and long afterwards Danish soil. Down till the days of Gustavus Adolphus the provinces in the South of the Scandinavian peninsula on the Eastern side belonged to Denmark; and Scania, between which and the Island of Zealand flows the Sound, was the Danish earldom of Strut-Harold, Sigvald's father.

The Viking captains, running first through the Sound between Rügen and the Wendish main, steered for a point in Scania, near which the modern town of Malmoe stands, and to do this they had to run between Falster and Moen, the islands which were to form part of Gunnhilda's dower

It was no part of Sigvald's plan to pay a

visit to his father Strut-Harold. They were to turn neither right nor left till they had landed King Sweyn safe and sound on his own land.

But as the King steered Sigvald's ship a little ahead of all the rest, the men on the watch on the forecastle called out as they ran between the islands,—

"Ships ahead! full fifty of them."

"Ships ahead!" said Sigvald; "then there is gain and spoil to be got. Hold on your course, King Sweyn."

On the Vikings came, and on board every ship the crews got ready for battle, for to them the odds of fifty to thirty were never counted.

A little while after the men on the forecastle called out again,—

"They row out to meet us in two lines."

"What shall we do, Sigvald?" said the King; "shall we hold on singly, or lash our ships together, and so await their onset?"

"Hold on singly," said Sigvald; "we cannot tell yet whether they are friends or foes."

"I thought all men were your foes," said Sweyn, "and that your hands were against all."

"Never against thee, King Sweyn, till the day that force drove me to it."

"Say no more of that, Sigvald," said the King. "Let bygones be bygones."

"I am loath to fight them," said Sigvald, "though they come on so boldly, and bear themselves with such a high hand. This is the only voyage I have ever been on which I hoped might end as it has begun in peace."

"But what be they?" said the King; "Swedes, or Northmen, or Russians. Have you not a man who can say which they be?"

"On the look-out are ten of the best sailors in the squadron," said Sigvald; "and if they cannot tell us no man can."

"Let some one hold the tiller and steer the ship," said the King; "and let us two go forward and scan the strangers."

So said so done; the King gave up the tiller to a trusty man, and he and Sigvald were soon on the forecastle gazing at the hostile squadron which was still at some distance off gliding in two lines through the still waters of the Sound.

"They be tall stout ships," said the King, as he gazed at them closely.

"Tall and stout indeed," said Sigvald. "Such as a man might wish rather to have on his side than against him. Northmen, too," he cried, "and no Russians, by their even rowing and their gallant trim."

"They look," cried King Sweyn, "strangely like my own ships, like the fifty I sent out this summer to harry Elthelred's coasts."

By this time the strangers had swept on nearer, and Sigvald cried out:

"True, king, these are Danish ships and none other. See, there is your crimson standard with the white cross at the mast-head, which the emperor gave your father. Now we shall meet them as friends and not foes."

On and on the two squadrons drew to each other, till the Vikings, who still held their straight course through the Sound, were between the two divisions of the Danes, and were almost within speaking distance.

Then ensued what, as Beorn afterwards said was worth coming all the way from Wales to see. Just as the Vikings were in mid-channel the Danish ships on either side of them turned their prows towards them and bore down on them at full speed so as to get them between what we should call two fires. There was just time for the Vikings if they had chosen to pull on and escape the onslaught, but King Sweyn now seized the tiller and turned the prow of Sigvald's ship towards the enemy, and in less time than it takes to describe the evolution the Viking squadron lay in a double line, fifteen facing one way and fifteen the other, ready to receive the foe. So there the two lay, fifteen against twenty-five on each side, and all men waited to see what would happen; nor did any one except those on board Sigvald's ship yet know the nationality of the strangers.

At last the two lines drew near, and as they got within hail the leader of the Danes called out:

"Who are ye who fare so unwarily through the Danish waters?"

"Vikings of Jomsburg," shouted Sigvald; "and if you must know why we fare so unwarily, it is because we look on these waters just as much ours as King Sweyn's."

"Know ye aught of King Sweyn?" hailed the captain. "We are on our way to Jomsburg to seek him."

"We know so much about him," said Sigvald, "that he is here with us on board this ship, which he now steers."

At these words which passed between Sigvald and the Danish Captain from the prow of either vessel, the word was passed on board the Danish ships to back their oars and to cease their preparations for attack. The Danish Captain shoved off a boat, boarded Sigvald's ship, and saw the King. Convinced of his safety the two fleets fraternized, and much as King Sweyn may have wished for revenge he had no opportunity of wreaking it at once.

That night the squadrons lay together in a creek in the Sound. Next morning the King and Queen went on board his own fleet and steered for Zetland, while the Vikings remained behind. As he parted from Sigvald, King Sweyn said;

"Thanks, Sigvald, Harold's son, for all your courtesy. The next time we meet I trust I may be able to repay you for what you have done for us."

CHAPTER XVIII.

BEORN AND VAGN GO A-SEA ROVING.

When the Danes sailed off triumphantly with their King, the Vikings remained behind, and Sigvald proposed that they should all return to Jomsburg. All agreed to this except Beorn, the Welshman, who said:

"You have to command, Captain, and we to obey; but if I may have my way, I and Vagn will go with our three ships on a short autumn cruize. To tell the truth, I have had enough of women and feasts. I long for the whining of the arrow in the air and for the hurtling of spears. Sweeter far to me is the scream of the sea-mew than the bleating of sheep. Let us stay behind, therefore, and go you all back to the burg: we shall be home long before the first winter night;" which we may inform the reader fell on the 26th of October.

"Go as you please or stay as you please,"

said Sigvald, "You and Vagn will do honour to the company whithersoever ye go. If ye fall, to us remains the blood-feud and the duty of revenge."

"Never fear for that, Sigvald," said Beorn; "the arrow is not yet feathered that shall be my bane, nor the spear-head forged that shall rattle through my ribs."

"Fare in peace then," said Sigvald; "we will all keep this Yule right jovially in Jomsburg."

So the rest of the squadron rowed back to the burg, while Beorn and Vagn and a captain of theirs, whose name was Wolf the Unwashed, remained in Bornholm Sound uncertain as yet whither to turn in search of spoil.

While their comrades sails could still be seen in the offing Beorn said to Vagn, "Right glad am I, foster-child, that they have left us here alone. Now we shall do some good that we are here together with three stout ships and three hundred stalwart men. But as for your fleets and squadrons, they frighten off chapmen and Vikings. You may get fame in a fleet but never fee. Sometimes to my mind spoil is better than glory."

"I do not think so," said Vagn; "I feel as if I had spoil enough and sigh for glory."

"What more glory could you wish for than to beat Sigvald and make him yield before you in arms. There's no satisfying some people. You are at the top of the tree, and instead of sitting there and plucking the fruit, you wish to stretch out to climb higher in the clouds and so down you will come with a fall."

All this time Wolf the Unwashed, so called because he seldom rejoiced in the pleasures of the bath, a huge raw-boned, brawny Viking stood by listening to their talk. When it was over he said to Beorn:

"Well, Master Beorn, which is it to be this time, gain or glory? Are we to lie in wait for chapmen, or fall on some Vikings like ourselves and spoil them? Whither shall we turn, too? Up East to Lifland or to Samland where the yellow amber lies thick on the shore, or to the Swedish Lakes or through the Sound 'to the Bay' where we were last spring when we spoiled Thorkell of Leira's goods."

"I am for the Bay," said Vagn with a blush.

"And I am not," said Beorn doggedly. "No!

no! we have had quite enough of that work. I will not go within a hundred miles of a woman if I can help it. Enough harm has been done already in that way this autumn. If we go to 'the Bay,' foster-child, you'll be putting your head into the wolf's den only for what, to catch a sight of Ingibeorg, Thorkell's daughter. This time we are out for adventures with men, and not for woman's love. Far sooner would I go back to Jomsburg without dipping oar in brine than to go hankering after the prettiest maid in the world."

"Just spoken to my mind," said Wolf; "I never could see the use of women. Why can't men be born as they were in old time, when one leg of Borr the giant rubbed itself against the other and out came a man. But ever since men have been born of women there has been naught but strife in the world."

"Strife," repeated Vagn indignantly; "and what would you be, Wolf, without strife? why, it is the bread you live on and the cup you drink. You ought to be the best friend of women in the world instead of being the worst."

"I mean another kind of strife," said Wolf;

"the strife I hate is what comes of woman's words and gabble, praising one man and abusing another, sowing discord with the tongue and ever reaping a fresh crop. That's the strife I hate, and it comes from women. Another kind of strife I like, and ever shall like, the strife of men, when swords clash in sweet music and red wounds rosier than the rose are given and taken. That is the strife I like, but as for the strife that comes from the backbiting and talebearing of women, that I cannot abide."

This was such a very eloquent speech from Wolf the Unwashed, that old Beorn jumped up and clapped him on the back and bawled out:

"Well spoken, unwashed one! I only wish such words had weight in Jomsburg; but, alas! the golden time is over with us Vikings. It is as if the peace of Asgard were gone for ever, and the Frost Giants and their hags come into the mansions of the gods."

Then while Vagn looked moodily on he said,—

"But all this is dry work. Let us have a horn of mead, and when we have washed the cobwebs out of our throats, we will settle what course we shall steer."

While the two topers dispatched their mead Vagn looked listlessly on. He was in a minority, and the hope that had flashed across his mind of seeing Ingibeorg again faded away. He could scarcely venture on an expedition against Thorkell of Leira with one ship, and so was bound to follow his companions in arms.

"There be nice creeks and bays all along the Swedish shore among the isles," said Wolf, "whither the chapmen from Russia betake them as they run down the Baltic in autumn. They will be as full of rich prizes just now as an open lake in winter is full of ducks. Let us try them, Beorn."

"With all my heart," said Beorn; "we want furs sadly for winter, and these Russian chapmen bring richer sables and fox-skins and ermine than ever Earl Hacon can get from his Finns and Lapps."

"Then there is amber and gold and honey and wax and fine linen and pell and Eastern wares, spoil to be had just for stretching out the hand."

"When shall we sail?" asked Vagn, as much for the sake of saying something as because he cared for the cruize.

"Sail!" said Beorn; "why this very minute. Why should we lie idle here when there's gain to be got on every side of us."

Up the West coast of the Baltic, therefore, they steered, that day and the next and the next till they had run through Calmar Sound and were off the coast of Gothland. But they scarce saw a sail bigger than a fishing boat, and Beorn and Wolf bewailed their ill luck in going so far and finding so little.

On the morning of the fourth day as the sun rose they again fell in with a fishing boat, and asked the crew for news, and if there were any chapmen thereabouts.

"Yes," said the men, "there was one ran into yonder creek last night, or, to tell the truth, five of them ran laden to the water's edge with goods. They would be an easy prey to your long-ships, for they were ill-manned."

This was such good news to the Vikings that they cleared the ships for action at once, and swept at full speed with their oars round the headland into the bay.

But the sight that met them there was hardly so agreeable as they expected. There up in the bight of the bay lay five ships indeed, but so far from being those of chapmen or traders, they were long-ships, of a size quite equal to any of their own, and at one glance they saw that the leader of the five was getting his ships under way to attack them.

"How say you, Vagn? How say you, Wolf?" hailed Beorn to his two comrades. "Shall we hold on or lash ourselves together and await their onslaught? For as to turning tail, I do not think any Viking of Jomsburg would think three against five too great odds."

"Lash ourselves together," was the answer; so they lashed their ships together in line, for which there was just time before the enemy came down on them.

When they came within hail, Beorn stood up on the forecastle of his ship, and called out:

"Who are ye that fare so boldly in this bay? See ye not that here are warships before you, and what is your leader's name?"

"Atli is my name, Earl Arnvid's son, of East Gothland, close by. But what men are ye?"

"We are our own men," said Beorn; "and, if you must know, we hail from Jomsburg."

"Then there is little love lost between us," said Atli. "Yield your ships or do battle."

"We Jomse-vikings," said Beorn, "never yield. 'Twere better that ye yielded yourselves; quit your ships and goods, and you shall have leave to go on shore. Else let the steel decide between us."

A haughty laugh from Atli was all the answer returned to this speech. On bore Atli with his five ships, and as he laid his galley alongside Beorn's, which lay on the starboard side, while Wolf's was in the middle and Vagn's on the larboard, the Earl snatched up a spear and hurled it among Beorn's crew. It was a good shot, and the Viking whom it struck met his death.

Then the battle became general, and the Swedes laid their vessels, which they had not lashed together, alongside and athwart the bows of the Viking's ships.

For some time the fight was carried on by missiles. Showers of stones and flights of spears and arrows flew from one side and the other, so that for some time it could not be seen which had the advantage in this kind of combat. At last, however, it was clear that the Vikings were the best marksmen, and that their shafts were gradually thinning the hostile crews.

Just then Atli made an attempt to carry Beorn's ship by boarding. His captain of the forecastle sprang up on the gunwale, leaped down on the gangway inside, and began to cut down all who stood before him. Four men fell by his hand before Beorn was aware of the danger. Then he rushed along the gangway to meet him. As he approached, Atli's man thrust at him with his spear, but Beorn held up his shield, and the blow passed through it ; and while his foeman was thus entangled, Beorn smote at him with his sword, and dealt him his death-blow. So he fell ; but he was now followed by Atli himself, who sprang on board Beorn's ship with a band of men.

All this time Wolf the Unwashed had remained idle, except in the war of missiles between the two ships to which his was lashed, but when he saw this fresh onslaught of Atli he sprang across the gunwale on to Beorn's ship, and called out :

"Up and at them, Beorn! all power to your arm this day."

"Powerful it is," said Beorn, as he smote down another of the foe; "but something tells me, Wolf, that you speak with a 'fey' mouth."

"'Fey,' or not 'fey,'" said Wolf, "a man can but die once," and as he said this he threw himself in Atli's way.

Just before they met, Wolf's foot slipped on the gangway, which was steeped in gore, and as he fell he laid himself open to Atli's attack, who at once thrust him through with his spear.

A shout from the Swedes behind Atli greeted the death of one of the Viking chiefs, and Atli and his men pressed on, and began to clear the gangway of the Vikings. The battle now seemed to hang in doubt, and Vagn, who was less pressed, now flew across Wolf's ship to the rescue of his foster-father. As he cleared the gunwale he found himself face to face with Atli, who smote at him with his sword, and clove his shield in twain down to the boss. While Vagn was brandishing his sword, seeking a bare place on Atli, a heavy stone discharged at random smote the Swedish leader on the left wrist and made him drop his shield. In another moment Vagn smote him just above the knee a mighty stroke and struck off his leg.

While Atli looked at the limb in wonder if it were really off, Vagn called out :

"Yes, Atli, so it is, your leg is off."

As he uttered these words he stabbed him through the body and gave him his death-blow.

Then Beorn and Vagn, shoulder to shoulder, turned on the rest of Atli's men who had boarded the ship, and drove them back to their own vessel. By this time so many of the Swedes had fallen on board their five ships that they had no heart to continue the struggle after the loss of their leader. They backed off, therefore, and then turned and fled up the bay.

"Shall they escape so, foster-father," said Vagn.

"By no means," said Beorn ; "cut our lashings asunder and let us press them home."

So said so done. In a little while the three Viking ships, with diminished crews, but spirits as bold as ever, were under way to attack their foes. As they rowed up it was only to see that the day was won already. The Swedes threw themselves out of their ships and left them, some in boats and some by swimming or wading to the land. The Vikings took possession of the abandoned vessels, and by midday Beorn and Vagn sat on the decks of their ships, weary and battle-worn indeed, but still masters of five ships and a great store of goods and spoil.

"Not a bad morning's work, foster-father," said Vagn.

"No," said Beorn; "but I would give up all my share could I bring Wolf the Unwashed to life again."

"So would I," said Vagn. "He was a brave Viking, and if ever a man deserved to win his way to Valhalla it was our comrade."

"We will bind our wounds and bathe our limbs to-day," said Beorn; "to-morrow we will land and bury our friend, as a Viking should be interred, after the ancient rites."

So they spent that day in rest and leech-craft, and slept that night in peace on board their ships, their late foes having fled into the woods, too scared to venture to attack them again.

CHAPTER XIX.

THE BURIAL OF THE VIKING.

SOME of our readers may, perhaps, feel inclined to inquire what became of Atli's body, and those of his followers who were slain on board Beorn's ship. On this point we can satisfy their curiosity. It was no part of the customs of that age to insult the body of a fallen foe. On the contrary, it was looked on as duty to bury it, and so the morning after the conflict those of the enemy who had fallen were taken on shore and interred. If any one supposes that the last duties to the dead were performed by "cremation," as it is the modern fashion to call it, it would be a mistake. Burning the dead had long ceased in the North when the events recorded in this story happened. That mode of burial went out with what ethnologists call the Bronze Age. We are now in the Iron Age, when swords and arrow-heads were of steel, and bodies were buried and not burnt.

Having disposed in this manner of their fallen foes, the Vikings turned their attention to their own men, of whom about twenty, including Wolf the Unwashed, had been slain. First, they washed their wounds and combed their long hair, and arrayed their limbs in their best attire, for it was supposed that when the dead reached the other world, and entered Valhalla, they would need their bravest array when they met the bravest and greatest of all the Northern race in Odin's hall. As they were thus laid out on the poop of Beorn's ship, each man had his axe and sword and spear by his side. A good archer had his bow and arrows handy, and under each corpse lay the oblong shield.

When these duties had been performed, Beorn and Vagn mustered their crews, and then a curious ceremony was performed. Though clad in their best, it might be remarked that the feet of the dead were shoeless.

Beorn now stood up and said :

"Ye good men and true, who listen to my

words, you all know that faiths now-a-days are much mixed. One man believes in Odin and the ancient Gods; another in the White Christ; another, like the Wends, in Peran, the God of Thunder; or in Bielbog, the God of Light; or in Czernebog, the Black God; and, last of all, there are some, and these not a few, of our company who believe in nothing but themselves and their good swords; for, in truth, what between priests and monks, Christian and heathen, no man knows what to believe. If this be so while men are alive, it is not so when they are dead. Men come into the world from darkness, like a bird that flies in at night through a warm, lighted hall, and out at the other end into darkness again. That is death. But because it is not good for a man not to know whither he is going when his life is done, we think it right to bury our slain after the old fashion, so that, as they have fallen like men in battle, they may now go to the God of Battles, who is ready to receive them into his hall."

Here Beorn paused, and the Vikings mur-

mured their assent, after their usual custom, to his words. Then he went on :

"We have dressed them in their bravest attire. By their sides lie their best arms, comely they all look in their wounds and in their death ; but one thing is wanting : bring hither the hellshoon, lads !"

At these words twenty-one pairs of shoes belonging to the dead were brought forward, and Beorn went on :

"We all know the meaning of this. First of all, these, our comrades, must walk on the way to Hela's house, deep down below nine worlds. That is the abode to which all the dead must first come, and stay there three days, till it is settled where they shall remain for ever ; the brave with Odin and Thor, and the coward with Hela, the grim goddess, the queen of thralls and cravens. None have ever gone on that way and returned, save Hermod the brisk, Odin's man, who rode on it to hear tidings of Balder, when Balder fell ; but we know that the path is rough and rugged, and that a man will need good shoon to his feet if he will fare to Hela. These shoon, then, we bind on our brothers' feet; for all who lie here are brothers by the law of the company."

After these words, Beorn, with the assistance of Vagn, put the shoes on each of the dead men's feet, taking Wolf last. This was the duty of a man's nearest relative; but in that band brotherhood in arms overbore the ties of blood; and Beorn, as captain, was looked on as nearer to each of the slain than their nearest relatives had they been present.

As he tied each shoe fast by its laces round the ankle of the corpse, he said:

"So I bind this hell-shoe, that it may last to Hela's house."

When he came to Wolf, he said, besides:

"I know not how to bind on a hell-shoe if this does not hold."

Then began what might be called the funeral procession. Four Vikings took up each body, raising it on the shield on which it lay, stiff and stark, and bore it down the sloping gangway to the shore.

There, on a little knoll, the ground had been levelled for the base of a cairn, large enough to hold the twenty bodies of the rank and file, as they might be called, which were arranged round that of Wolf the Unwashed, though now well washed in his death, which lay in the middle in the place of honour.

When each had been thus reverently laid on earth, a trench was dug round the knoll, so as to form a deep ditch, and the excavated earth was heaped up over the dead, till they were buried about four feet deep. Then the last rites were looked on as over; and the Vikings went back to their ships.

As Beorn walked slowly away with Vagn, he said:

"It cuts me to the heart that we had no time to bury Wolf, the bravest of men, like a true Viking, in his own ship, under a cairn. This is but a scurvy burial after all."

"No man need grieve," said Vagn, "if at any time he does the best he can. We had no time to do more, and Wolf and the rest must be content. They will not think worse of him in Odin's hall—if there be such a hall—that he comes there without his ship; for the Valkyries, who choose the slain in all fights, well know how many brave warriors Wolf the

Unwashed has sent in his time to the banquets of Valhalla."

"It is true," said Beorn, "we have done our best, and the best can do no more. The cairn, too, looks high enough, and in days to come no man will know how we eked out its height by turning a little knoll into a cairn."

All that afternoon time hung heavy on the hands of the Vikings. The funeral ceremonies still weighed on their minds; and, in spite of the strong ale and mead, in which they drank heirship to Wolf and the fallen, dividing their goods among the crews. Beorn felt that something was needed to restore the spirits of the men.

"What think you," he said to Vagn, "of marching up the country to-night, and seeing what spoil we can find? Somewhere hereabouts is the temple of the Eastern Goths; and, if we hit upon it, we might find ample treasure."

"But can we rob a temple?" asked Vagn. "Have we not just buried our dead with the rites of the ancient Gods?"

"Temples," said Beorn, sententiously, "were

made to be robbed! They ever have been robbed in my time, and ever will be. Why, we had a priest, not so long ago, in Jomsburg, that same shaveling, who told his beads and sang his hymns so dolefully, who said the ancient Gods were but idols, and that no God lived in temples made with hands."

"It goes against me to spoil the temples of the Gods," said Vagn; "but if all the band will go, I will not stay behind."

"We will put it to the men, then," said Beorn. "Poor fellows, they need something to keep up their hearts. That Atli and his followers fight well."

So Beorn went about the crews, and found, as he had expected, that they had no scruples of the kind which hampered Vagn's mind. One said he thought it as little harm to rob a temple as to burn a church; and he had often burned the churches of the Christians away in the West. Another said he would not burn a temple, though he did not mind easing their idols of their useless goods; another thought if the idols were really gods, they would know how to defend themselves. The end of it all was, that the Vikings agreed to go that nigt in search of the temple of the Eastern Goths; what they might do when they found it, and had accomplished the adventure, was another thing. Perhaps they might neither burn nor sack the temple after all.

So at nightfall they set out, one hundred picked men, the rest being left to mind the ships, and keep open the line of retreat. As they passed along a path through the thick pine forest, about as bewildering as the Ashantee bush, Beorn said to Vagn:

"This wood is like a man's life, foster-child; no one can tell when and where it will end."

As he said this, an arrow whirred through the air, and one of the band behind fell dead, stricken in the throat.

"There ended one," said Vagn; "and yet the wood has not ended."

"On, on!" said Beorn. "I see a clearing ahead. If we reach that, we shall, at least, see the hand that launches these shafts."

A moment after, one of the band behind called out:

"We have caught the man who shot the arrow, if it be fair to call him a man."

"Bring him hither," said Beorn. "Let me scan him by the moonbeams," for we have forgotten to say that it was at the full.

So the baneman of the Viking was brought to the front, and found to be a boy of scarce ten years old, whose puny arm seemed scarce able to draw the bow which he had used so well.

"Speak," said Beorn, sternly. "What drove thee to slay one of our band, against whom thou hadst no quarrel?"

"Did one of you fall to my shot?" said the boy. "Then I have avenged my father."

"How say you that?" said Beorn. "When slew we your father, or any of your kin?"

"Two nights since," said the boy, "he fell with Atli, Arnvid's son, in fight with you Vikings. All day have I been watching you in the wood to take my revenge."

"Spoken like a man," said Vagn, "though you be but a boy. Beorn, we can never take such a child's life. Let him have peace; for, after all, he only avenged his father, and the blow fell nearest to him."

"He shall have peace," said Beorn; "but he must do something towards an atonement. He shall show us the way to the temple which we seek."

"What is your name, lad?" said Vagn. "It is ill speaking with a nameless man."

"My name is Grim," said the boy. "Grim Askel's son, that Askel whom ye slew yestermorn, and whom I have now avenged."

"Will you take peace of me, Grim?" said Vagn; "and will you do something for us to save your life?"

"That depends," said the boy, "on what that something is; there be things which I could not do to save my life."

"Spoken like a good and true man again," said Vagn, kindly. "We seek the temple of the Eastern Goths, which lies somewhere near; will you guide us to it?"

The boy paused for a moment, while a smile played across his face in the bright moonbeams, and then said:

"Yes, Vikings; I will guide you to the temple."

"Lead on then," said Beorn; "and remember, Grim, that your life is forfeited already. At the least sign of guile or treachery, I strike you dead with this axe."

This threat, strange to say, seemed to fall on idle ears. All that the boy said was:

"Yes; I see it is a broad and bitter axe. No doubt many have had their death-blow at its edge. Hath it a name, pray, Captain?"

"I call it the 'Ogress of War,'" said Beorn. "Two nights ago some of you Easterlings felt her edge."

"Indeed!" said the boy; and on he went before Beorn.

So they passed through wood after wood, and clearing after clearing, seeing no houses until their patience began to fail, and then the Vikings asked how far they had still to trudge.

"Are there no houses in this land?" said Vagn to Grim.

"None," said the boy. "I thought it was not houses, but temples, that ye wished to find?"

"So we do," said Beorn. "Bring us speedily to the temple, or—" And as he said this he raised his axe.

"Can I bring the temple nearer than it is?' asked Grim. "You Vikings, I know, are so strong, and can do anything. I am but a boy, and must do what I can, and that is but little."

"But is it near this temple?" asked Vagn.

"Not far off now," said Grim. "Not more than five bowshots beyond this next belt of wood."

"Let us haste towards it," said Beorn. "The night is wearing out, and it is as far back as hither."

"So it is," said the boy.

The Vikings reached the belt, and soon crossed it. As they came into the open space beyond, Grim pointed to a building, partly hidden in the mist, which clung to the ground.

"Behold the temple, the only temple that I know of in these parts."

"The temple! the temple!" shouted the Vikings, as they dashed forward into the open space.

As they drew nearer to the building, Beorn said:

"If it be a temple, 'tis the strangest one I ever saw, though I own I do not know much of temples either outside or in. But if I called it anything, I should say it was a wooden church, for all the world like those I used to see and to worship in away in Wales, my native land."

"What you call a church we call a temple," said Grim. "We are all Christians in this part of East Gothland, since Anschar came."

"And who is Anschar?" asked Vagn, while Beorn and the Vikings paused in their course.

"Anschar is a priest from England," said Grim. "He has been here ever since I can remember, and has built this temple to the Christians' God, and made us all Christians hereabouts, so to speak."

In the meantime, Beorn and the Vikings had recovered their surprise to find that, while seeking for a temple, they had fallen on a church.

"What is the difference between a temple and a church?" asked he that had owned to burning of churches in the West. "In both there is silver, and sometimes gold. Both are the fair spoil of such Vikings as us."

Then the Vikings dashed on, dragging Grim with them.

But as they neared the church, they heard

the strains of solemn music and of hymns chanted in the little building. At the same time they remarked that lights shone through the narrow slits which served as windows.

"Be the priests in this temple up and stirring at this hour?" asked Beorn of Grim. "If they were honest men they would be in their beds."

"But are you not honest men?" retorted Grim; "and are ye in your beds?"

"Do they always rise so early?" asked Vagn.

"They are always in church at this hour," said Grim, "and they call it Lauds or 'Praises'—that is how they begin the day, with prayers and hymns."

"Shavelings and cowards!" said Beorn. "Let us break into the church, and scatter them and their praises to the four winds, and sack the church of everything it contains worth carrying away."

"You will find little in it worth spoiling," said Grim. "These priests are poor indeed, and live by the labour of their own hands. All these clearings in the wood were made by them.

Since they have been here we have never had dearth in East Gothland, for they sow wheat, and rye, and oats, and their harvests are always good."

"And, Grim," asked Beorn, as they neared the church door, "when the harvests fail do you burn the priests in their church, as the Swedes do their kings, in time of dearth?"

"I tell you since Anschar has been here the harvests have been ever good," said Grim; "but see, the door opens, and he comes out to meet you."

As he spoke, out of the church came first a band of choristers, singing a sweet hymn, and then incense-bearers swinging their censers, which gave out the perfume of frankincense, so strange to the nostrils of the Vikings. Then came Anschar himself, followed by his priests and deacons, all in their holy vestments, and all chanting the same solemn strain.

As they advanced a sort of panic-fear seized the rude Vikings, and even Beorn himself recoiled before the advance of the Christian clergy.

Whether it was that Anschar was aware of

their approach, and had come out thus to meet them in the hope of arresting their wrath, or whether he thought it was a crowd of the inhabitants of the country who had gathered together thus early to worship at the church, is uncertain. What is sure is, that he, by a most happy thought, came out thus boldly to meet the invaders, and so took them at a great disadvantage by the suddenness and solemnity of his movements.

Slowly but surely the white-robed band advanced against the armed array of the Vikings, who, as they came closer, opened on either side to make way for them till Anschar stood face to face with Grim, and Beorn, and Vagn.

Then the singing ceased, and Anschar, in a still low voice, so different from the rude shouts and hailing of the Vikings, said to Beorn :

"God's peace be with thee, noble Captain. Come ye thus early to worship at our church ?"

Beorn clutched his axe with uneasy fingers, as though he was itching to cleave the holy man to the chine, and some of the Vikings drew their swords and waited for a signal to strike down the Christians and sack the church. But no such signal came. Beorn, bold as he was, quailed before the clear cold gaze of the priest, and with faltering tongue he said :

"You bid us God's peace ; but it is on war rather than peace that we come."

"War !" said Anschar. "Why war with us? We are not men of war, but men of peace. We bring peace in God's name to all the world, and to you and your band among the rest."

Still Beorn quailed and winced before him, but he would not yield till he had made another effort.

"I tell you again, priest, we are men of war and not of peace. War is the breath of life in our nostrils. I tell you we came to sack your church, and to slay you all if you resist, and not to worship to your idols with that strange savour in our nostrils."

"Slay us if you will," said Anschar ; "we will not resist ; not one of us would lift his hand against you. But sack not nor burn the church, for it is God's house, and on him that takes aught from God the wrath of God will surely fall."

"You speak," said Beorn, "like the priests I

heard when I was a boy, not so big as this lad here, and your words have a strange sound, as an echo of things long since forgotten. So sang and so spoke the priests in my father's house at Deganwey in Wales."

At these words Anschar looked at Beorn and said: "Are you British, and not Norse, by birth? and what was your father's name?"

"His name," said Beorn, impatiently, but with the air of a man who felt forced to answer even against his will, "his name was Howel, Howel the Good. He was lord of seven cantreds, and some of that rule is still mine by right. My mother's name was Githa, daughter of a Norse sea-king, and though a Welshman born, that was why I was called Beorn. But why, priest, do you ask so closely after my lineage?"

"Because I, too," answered Anschar, "have been at Deganwey, in the good old times, in the hall of Howel the Good. His soul is with the saints, I trust; and here I, a missionary from the Anglo-Saxon Church, meet his son in East Gothland, and he tells me he will sack my church and spoil God of his goods."

"It is the way of the world," said Beorn, bitterly. "Every man makes the bed on which he must lie. Had my father lived I had been now, no doubt, a Prince and a Christian in Wales, but I went early out sea-roving with my grandfather, and one autumn, when we came back from our cruise, we found that a band of Vikings from Scotland had landed on the fair sands of Conway, and had slain my brother, and carried off my mother, and sacked Deganwey, the strong castle, and only left me the wasted land and starving folk. Then I took to the sea, and harried the coasts of Scotland east and west, and forsook the Christian faith, and took to that of the Northmen, and now, as many of us here will tell you, we halt between two faiths, and know not which to believe. The old Gods have no power, and as for your new white Christ, he seems too craven and contemptible for any Viking to trust in."

"The day will come," said Anschar, solemnly, "when not only you Vikings, but every man in the North, aye, and though it be far to see, when every man on this middle-earth will believe in Christ, as I and these babes do, and when there shall be but one God and one faith in all the world."

As he uttered these words, with a prophetic fervour, he spread his arms wide abroad, as though embracing the Vikings, who shrank from him, while they gazed on him as it were spell-bound.

Anschar saw his opportunity, and went on :

"It was well that ye came thus early, for it is the day of the Holy Saint Michael the Archangel, and after this procession, in which ye will join, we will all worship in the church, and thou Beorn at least wilt renew the orisons of thy youth."

As he spoke, Anschar gave the word to the choristers, and the incense-bearers moved on. Beorn and the Vikings—half in jest, half in earnest—joined in the train, and the end of that early meeting was, that those who went out to burn and kill remained, if not to worship with the Christians, at least to be spectators of their service.

The church was filled to overflowing, and such lauds had never been celebrated within its walls before. The Vikings sat the service out in gloomy wonder at the solemnity of the ceremonies, the splendour of the vestments, the sweet fragrance of the incense, and the brilliancy of the lights.

When it was over, Anschar said to Beorn before they left the church: "Ye came out to rob and spoil. See what there is in our sacristy worth taking. A man, were he to lose his soul, might lose it for things of greater price."

As he uttered these words, he led Beorn towards the little cupboard in the sacristy, which contained their church plate. A chalice of latten, a patin of the same, and a flagon of brass were all their goods.

"If you wish for spoil from churches you must go where Christianity is older," said Anschar. "There you may find silver and gold and gems. In Sweden Christianity is too young to be rich, and even our vestments, though outwardly splendid, would be not worth your long march to take."

"One thing we need," said Beorn, "if we may have it, and that is food and drink."

"Both ye shall have and willingly," said Anschar. "That is, bread and flesh, ale and mead, we have none, and never taste; but if milk and cream will serve your wants, of these we have ample store."

"We were unworthy the name of Vikings," said Beorn, "if we needed ale and mead every day. In this world a man must take what he can get."

So the Vikings were fed on the best that the priests could furnish, and at daybreak they were ready to return to their ships. Before they went Anschar said to Beorn:

"One thing, Beorn, Howel's son, I beg of thee, and that is what thou mayst well grant, in that I, all unworthy though I be, by the grace of God, have saved thee from the commission of mortal sin."

"What is that?"

"The life of this boy Grim," said Anschar. "He has guided thee back to Christ, and who knows if the seed sown on this, St. Michael's day, may not spring up in some of your hearts for good."

"He has slain one of our men," said Beorn, "and his life is due by all the laws of the blood-feud to the band."

"But he was a true and faithful guide," said Vagn, "and besides he only did what he was bound to do in avenging his father."

"Not so! not so!" cried the priest, "it is an idle and a wicked custom, and clean against God's will, who says, 'Vengeance is mine; I will repay, saith the Lord.'"

"What atonement can he offer to the band for their brother," said Beorn, doggedly.

"None, "said Anschar; "the boy hath neither kith nor kin now that his father is gone; but I can offer an atonement for him, and that is the blood already shed for every man on the Cross, the blood of our Lord and Saviour Jesus Christ. That atonement I can offer, and that blood far outshines in worth the lives of all the peoples of the earth."

"But how do you offer it?" asked Beorn.

"In the Blessed Sacrament of the Body and Blood of Christ."

"I do not understand thee," said Beorn, "though methinks I have heard something before, as it were in a dream. But to show thee that I value thy prayer, and in memory of the days when I was a Christian in my father's hall,

I will give thee the life of this boy, and I, myself, will pay to the band the full price of a man in atonement for the comrade we have lost."

"Spoken like a noble chief," said Anschar, "and now Grim you belong to me."

"With all my heart," said the boy, as he flew to the priest's side. "Now I will be as thou art, and slay no more men."

Then the priest and the Vikings parted, and Beorn and his men marched back to their ships through the wood. On their arrival they found that nothing had happened during their absence. But if we must say it, those who returned had to bear many jests from those who stayed behind. "Who ever heard," they said, "of men going out to rob a temple, and finding it, and, yet returning without a penny's worth of spoil."

CHAPTER XX.

BEORN AND VAGN GO BACK TO JOMSBURG.

On the 1st of October, two days after the day of St. Michael, the Vikings set off on their return to Jomsburg. The day before they shared the spoil which they had found on board of Atli's five ships. Though not a man, alive or dead or wounded, had been left on board, there was great store of goods robbed from all the chapmen, which that Viking had been able to board.

There were in fact all those costly Eastern wares and silken stuffs which Beorn had before mentioned, as likely to fall in their way. Amber from the Livonian and Prussian coasts; gold and silver rings from Russia; honey, mead, ale, and arms.

All these were brought to "the Pole," as it was called; that is, to the Standard Pole, that they might be shared or sold for the common good. Everything was then portioned into ten lots: one of which went to Sigvald, the Captain of the band; two were reckoned the portion of the company itself; and one lot went to the captain of each ship; and the other six were equally divided amongst the crews.

When all was over, Beorn said to Vagn, "This has not been so bad an autumn cruise. How good it was of Atli to save us the trouble of collecting it from each of the chapmen."

"It has been a profitable cruize indeed," said Vagn; "but what shall we do with the ships, we have not men enough to man them and take them home."

"No," said Beorn; "then they must go the way of all ships at last—either to be sunk in the water or burnt in the flames. To Ran or to Loki all wood comes at last, and these timbers shall go both ways at once. The Goddess of the Sea shall have her share, and the God of Fire his. We will set them on fire as they lie, and when they have burnt to the waters' edge, the hulks will sink to the bottom, and the sea will have her spoil."

That very night Anschar and his priests and acolytes were astonished at a great glare towards the coast, and sent the swift-footed Grim out to spy and bring back news. Through the woods the boy watched the flames, as they devoured the trim ships on which his father had sailed. Then towards dawn, when the flames grew low, each hull blazed up for a moment, and then sank to the bottom with a dull hissing sound. When all was dark again, he stole back through the black forest and brought word to Anschar.

"It was only Beorn and his Vikings amusing themselves with burning Atli's ships."

Next day the Vikings started on their three days' voyage to Jomsburg. Three days and nights, as they reckoned, would bring them home if the weather were fine; and finer morning never smiled on man than that on which they made their way out of the mesh of islands which fringed the coast of East Gothland and ran out into the open Baltic.

So the weather continued till they reached Calmar Sound, and were running between the Swedish main and Oland.

Early in the morning, when Beorn came on deck, and took the tiller from the old sea-dog who had steered the ship through the last watch, he looked round the sky, as all sailors are wont, and then growled a little and shook his head.

"You may well shake your head, Beorn," said the sailor. "We shall shake all over all of us ere the day be over."

It was dead calm, and there was a low haze which hung to the coast on either side, and distorted natural objects in a mirage or *Fata Morgana.* Headlands were inverted, rocks seemed double, trees stood on their crowns in the water with their trunks in the air. Everything was disturbed and turned upside down. Overhead was a great bank of cloud coming up against the little wind that blew in flaws as though it could never find strength to blow across the deep more than a dozen yards.

"Aye, aye," said Beorn, "our timbers will soon shake as well as our heads. Here is a tempest and a gale coming up, and it will be on us in no time; and now that we have passed Calmar Bay, there is never a haven to run for on this iron-bound coast."

"Bad weather for long-ships, Beorn," said the old sea-dog. "Now if this were a ship of burden, short, and round, and deep, we might ride like a nut-shell over the waves ; but what can one do with one of these long, narrow craft but stand by her till she breaks her back, and then make up one's mind to sleep in the sea caves with Ran."

"Not quite so bad as that, I hope," said Beorn. "I hope still to bear my bones back to my native land, and not to leave them by Baltic side. But this is the time to do, and not to talk. Put the ship about while I hail Vagn, and say what I mean to do."

The old sailor took the tiller, bade the rowers back to starboard and give way to larboard. Round flew the ship, while, as they turned, Vagn and the other vessel came up close on their quarter.

"Whither away now, foster-father," he shouted. "Back to East Gothland to look for Atli's and Wolf's bones."

Back to where Calmar Bay opens into the Baltic, our only shelter against the coming storm. Follow my lead, and put your ship about."

"Were I you," said Vagn, "I would hold on till every oar snapped in the row-locks, and till the mast came toppling down. Why be afraid of a cap full of wind, which, after all, may never come."

The words were scarce out of his mouth when the black clouds over their heads broke, and there was a flash of forked lightning, which seemed to run along the water, and plough up its smooth face. Then down came the rain in torrents, and out blew the wind in their teeth. In the narrow sound, where the water was pent up between the high shore on either side, the waves began to roll at once; and, as to Vagn's notion of holding on, it was confuted by the fact that it was only with the greatest difficulty, that he and his comrades succeeded in accomplishing the simple manœuvre which Beorn had just effected.

As it was, each ship broke several oars on either broadside, and shipped a deal of water, and was altogether in a crippled state.

"Now, give way with a will," shouted Beorn over the roaring of the wind and sea. "We must run before the storm, and try to make Calmar Bay, but it will be as much as we can do in this sea, where long-ships can scarcely live."

So the three ships ran before the wind, which sent great waves after them, threatening to poop them every moment. It was literally a race for their lives, and the three ships cut the water with awful speed.

And now the opening into Calmar Bay began to show itself. This was the most delicate operation of the whole, for the way in was fringed with reefs and rocks a-wash, and right in mid-channel was a shoal over which the breakers broke furiously. Added to this, the three ships had now to change their course, and to bring themselves broadside to the wind, which exposed them, but only for a short time, to the full force of the storm.

On this occasion as ever Beorn led; his was the post of danger; he was first to run the gauntlet of those shoals and that raging surf.

"Follow me close," he roared to the others. "I know the way in well—I could find it in the dark."

On he went, making the men ease their oars on the windward side, and pull with redoubled force on the lee. It was a near thing, but he contrived to run his ship in in safety ; and in a moment, after passing the shoal in mid-channel, was, so to speak, in smooth water, and able to look back on those that followed him. He had not to wait long. Next to him came Vagn, whose crippled ship was harder to steer.

"He will clear it," cried Beorn ; "the boy will clear it."

But he did not. Just then the wind seemed to blow spitefully with twofold force. Vagn's ship was driven on the shoal to leeward, and in a moment or two seemed to double up like matchwood as she took the ground. Worse still, her comrade, in trying to give her a wide berth, was thrown on the rocks on the opposite side.

"Both gone, both gone," said Beorn. "Two tall ships, and so many bold men. But launch the boat, lads ; she will live in this smooth water ;" and, with that, the hardy veteran threw himself into the skiff, that danced up and down on what he called the smooth water, and rowed as near as he could under the lee of the shoal on which Vagn's ship had split, but still clung together at the forecastle, which was hoisted high up into the air, and over which the waves broke incessantly.

As they reached the spot, Beorn's quick eye recognised the form of his foster-child clinging to the figure-head amidst the gleaming water.

"Back up," he cried, "as close as you can to the shoal on the leeward side."

This was done; and, to Beorn's delight, he saw that Vagn had seen their boat. It was of no avail to shout, but Beorn beckoned to him what to do. His last chance was to throw himself from the figure-head, and to try to fight his way through the raging surf into the still water beyond.

With a superhuman effort Vagn threw himself into the waves. A little while and he seemed lost, but at last he emerged beyond the line of surf, and was drifted, battered and breathless, to Beorn's boat.

"Take him up tenderly," said Beorn. "There is life in him yet, and, in saving him, we have saved the boldest heart in Jomsburg."

Three days afterwards Beorn and Vagn reached the castle, and were welcomed as those who had escaped out of the very jaws of death.

They had not returned as triumphantly as they hoped, but though the Vikings mourned their lost comrades and their tall ships, they felt consoled when they thought things might have gone far worse, for they might have lost as well Beorn the Welchman, and Vagn Aki's son, both of whom all agreed Jomsburg could never spare.

END OF VOLUME I.

BRADBURY, AGNEW & CO., PRINTERS, WHITEFRIARS

Milton Keynes UK
Ingram Content Group UK Ltd.
UKHW040928180224
437992UK00003B/93